Love, Hannah

From Bestselling Author
STACI HART

Copyright © 2017 Staci Hart

All rights reserved.
www.stacihartnovels.com

No part of this publication may be reproduced, distributed, or transmitted in any form or by any means, including photocopying, recording, or other electronic or mechanical methods, without the prior written permission of the publisher, except in the case of brief quotations embodied in critical reviews and certain other noncommercial uses permitted by copyright law. This book is a work of fiction.

Names, characters, places, and incidents either are products of the author's imagination or are used fictitiously. Any resemblance to actual persons, living or dead, events, or locales is entirely coincidental.

Cover by **Quirky Bird**
Editing by **Jovana Shirley, Unforeseen Editing**
Book design by **Inkstain Design Studio**
Proofreading by **Love N Books**

Playlist: http://spoti.fi/2y2vJK7

*To those who have sought
a place to call home.*

Love, Hannah

Wanted

HANNAH

This time, it will be different.

I repeated the thought as I had a hundred times that afternoon, hoping the words were more than wishful thinking. When I glanced down one final time to check the address written on the heavy paper, my heart skipped in my chest.

On the other side of the Victorian brownstone's door was a man who had lost his nanny without warning. I'd left my last au pair job in a rush that left me in limbo, and without another job, I'd lose my visa. And I wasn't quite ready to give up and go home. Not yet.

Another jolt of nerves raced up my back. The employment pairing by the agency had been hasty and thoughtless. I should have refused the moment I'd learned he was single. If I took the job, I'd have to move in with him for a year. I'd be alone with him, sharing his space, after swearing I wouldn't put myself in a position like the one I'd just walked away from. But I had no options. Things had happened too suddenly to plan for, and the opening at the Parker residence had popped up at the exact right moment.

So, there I was, standing on the doorstep of a beautiful home off Central Park, gambling on my future.

I summoned a long breath from deep in my lungs. I'd be smarter this time. And, if I caught even the slightest scent of danger in the air, I would refuse the job, simple as that.

Still, my heart tightened, thumping as I rang the doorbell.

It stopped completely when the door opened. For a moment, my fears washed out of me, fool that I was.

The first time I saw Charlie Parker, I didn't see one thing at a time; I saw all of him. It was an assault on my senses, an overwhelming tide of awareness, and for a moment, the details came to me in flashes over what was probably only a few seconds but felt so much longer.

His hair was blond and gently mussed, his face long and nose elegant. I could smell him, clean and fresh with just a touch of spice I couldn't place. I tipped my chin up—he was tall, taller than me, and I hovered just at six feet—and met his eyes, earthy and brown and so deep. So very deep.

And then he smiled.

He was handsome when he wasn't smiling. He was stunning when he was.

I was so lost in that smile, I didn't register the flying gob until it whapped against my sweater. Tiny splatters of something cold speckled my neck.

This was the moment the clock started again, and the sweet serenity slipped directly into chaos.

A blond little boy looked up at me from his father's side with a devilish gleam in his dark eyes. The spoon in his hand was covered in blood-red jam and aimed at me like an empty catapult.

Several things happened at once. Charlie's face morphed into embarrassed frustration as he reached for who I presumed to be his son. The boy—Sam, I guessed from the names I'd been given by the agency—spun around lightning fast and took off down the hallway, giggling. Another child began to cry from somewhere back in the house, and a bowl clattered to the ground, followed by a hissed swear from what sounded like an older woman.

I glanced down at the sliding, sticky mess against my white sweater and started to laugh.

Charlie's head swiveled back to me, his face first colored with confusion, then in horror as he looked at the Pollock painting on my sweater.

"Oh my God," he breathed, his apologetic, wide eyes dragging down my body. "Jesus, I am so sorry."

I was still laughing, almost a little hysterical. I couldn't even tell you why.

I waved a hand at Charlie, and he took my elbow, guiding me into the house as I caught my breath. Another crash came from the kitchen, and a little girl came toddling out into the entry, leaving powdery footprints on the hardwood.

Charlie's face screwed up. *"Sam!"* he called, stretching the word, a drawn-out promise of consequences.

A riot of giggling broke out in the kitchen.

We both snapped into motion. I followed him as he scooped up his crying daughter and stormed toward the kitchen. The little girl watched me over his shoulder with big brown eyes, her breath hitching in little shudders and her small finger hooked in her mouth.

Charlie stopped so abruptly, I almost ran into him.

When I looked around him and into the kitchen, my mouth opened. I covered it with my fingers as laughter bubbled up my throat.

A bag of flour sat in the middle of the floor, the white powder thrown in bursts against the surrounding surfaces and hanging in the air like smoke. The floor next to the bag was the only clean spot, shaped like a small bottom—the little girl's, I supposed. A bowl lay upside down, its contents oozing from under the rim and slung in a ring from ceiling to cabinet to floor, as if it had completed a masterful flip on its way to its demise. And in the center of the madness stood an older woman with flour in her dark hair and dusted down the front of her. Clutched under her arm was a wriggling Sam, offending spoon still in hand.

Her face was kind but tight with exasperation. "Please tell me this is the new nanny," she said flatly.

"I doubt we could convince her to stay at this point," he said with equal flatness.

He turned to me with a look that I could only describe as shame. But I smiled and reached for Maven.

Surprised, he gratefully handed her over. But when he turned for Sam, it was with thunder at his back.

Sam stopped kicking. His face turned to his father, eyes goggling and little mouth opened as a glob of jam dripped onto the floor and into the flour with a pat. Charlie relieved the woman of Sam and blew past me.

"Excuse me for one second, Hannah," he muttered before disappearing up the stairs.

I turned back to the older woman, whose face had softened. She brushed an errant hair from her face and sighed, wiping her hands on a dish towel that she slung over her shoulder as she approached.

Her smile was warm, as was her hand when I took it.

"*I'm sorry* just won't quite cut it," she said. "I'm Katie. And you must be Hannah."

"It's nice to meet you." I shifted Maven on my hip and reached for the paper towels. "Whatever happened?"

Katie sighed and walked over to the broom closet, coming back with the tool of the same name. "Thirty seconds, just long enough for Charlie to answer the door—that's all it takes with these two. I'd just turned my back—I was making roux for a sauce, and you can't stop stirring, or it burns—and Maven here retrieved the flour I'd just put away. Then, Sammy made thief's work of the jelly. You know the rest."

"Yes, I think I do," I said on a small laugh as I tried to wipe up Maven, though I only succeeded in spreading the mess around. "In Holland, we have a saying that goes, *Een kinderhand is snel gevund.* A child's hands are easily filled. In this case, with flour, I'd say."

Katie laughed, a friendly sound. "I have to agree. I suppose I should move it off the bottom shelf in the pantry." Her smile fell when she saw the front of me. "Oh, Hannah," she said like she'd single-handedly failed me, "what a mess Sammy made. Your sweater!"

I waved her off, though I did grab another paper towel, using it to mop up the excess that had slid a small distance down the knit fabric. "It's all right. It'll wash."

"Well, let me at least get you something to put on that." She stepped into a small room off the kitchen, returning with a little detergent patch in a packet.

"Thank you."

"It's the least I can do," she said, going back to the broom. "I'm the cook and housekeeper. Been here since just after Charlie's wife left," she said openly and without discretion, catching me off guard. "We *had* a nanny," she continued, "but she left last week for a family emergency. Jenny's about my age, and her widowed sister is real sick. But she left Charlie in a lurch—not quite fair, if you ask me. I'm happy to help out since she's been gone, but as you can see, I'm not quite qualified."

Katie motioned to the kitchen with a genial, if not a little deprecating, look on her face. It was just her way, I realized—the openness—and I found I rather liked it.

She sighed and set the broom aside, picking up the bowl from the ground. "Guess I'm starting my cornbread over again."

I chuckled. "Do you like working here?"

Katie beamed at that. "Oh, I do. Charlie's a good man even though he works harder than Noah building the ark. He tries; he does. We all see it. It helps that he's kind and generous. My last boss was a real piece of work."

"I can relate." I turned my full attention to Maven, taking care in cleaning her up as she looked up at me with bottomless brown eyes. "And the kids?"

That question elicited a sigh. "It's been bad since Jenny left. Better than when their mom left but still not great. It's not their fault, nor is it his. They just want their daddy, that's all. And Charlie doesn't have the time he wishes he had to give them. They're good kids, and Charlie does the best he can." She closed off the topic as footsteps sounded behind me.

I turned to find a freshly clothed Sammy, slope-shouldered and staring at his feet. Charlie stood behind him, brows low and with a hint of defeat in his eyes when they met mine.

He ushered Sammy forward. "Go on, son."

Sammy stepped toward me, eyes still down, hands in front of him. "I'm sorry," he said so pitifully, my heart ached.

I set Maven on the ground, and she toddled over to her father.

I knelt down to get level with Sammy. "That's quite all right. Just a bit of fun, yes?"

He sniffled. "Daddy's mad."

"Yes, well, it *was* very naughty, wasn't it?"

He nodded.

"And you made quite a mess of my sweater."

Sammy chanced a glance up at me, and I held his dark eyes.

"But it will wash, and you've told me you're sorry. Might we be friends now?"

Another nod—this one with a small, hopeful smile.

"I'm Hannah."

I offered my hand, and he took it firmly, his smile blooming.

"I'm Sammy. How come you talk funny?"

"Sammy," Charlie warned.

I looked up and saw he was embarrassed. "It's all right," I said to both of them. "I'm from Holland. Do you know where that is?"

Sammy shook his head.

"Have a look." In the flour on the floor, I drew a rough likeness of North America and made a dot on New York. "We're here, but I'm from here." I drew Britain and a bit of Europe, making another dot in the Netherlands. "Have you ever been to the beach, Sammy?"

He lit up. "I love the beach! We went to Coney Island once."

"Well, if you got in a boat and went a very long way, all the way across the ocean, you'd find yourself close to where I'm from."

"Could I swim there?"

I laughed. "No, it's much too far to swim. The fastest way is to fly in an airplane. But the reason I talk funny is because I'm Dutch. I speak Dutch, but I also know English, French, and Spanish."

He lit up. "How do you say"—he looked around the room—"chair?"

"Stoel."

He giggled. "Say dishes!"

"Borden."

"Say Katie!"

I laughed. "Katie."

Charlie stepped behind him, and I stood, finding myself a little short of breath at the sight of him smiling, his eyes flickering with failure, daughter in the crook of his arm and son's shoulder under his palm. There was something very honest about the sight, something dangerously disarming, and I found myself hoping I could stay.

"I'm so sorry, Hannah."

"It's no problem, Mr. Parker."

His cheeks flushed. "Please, call me Charlie. I don't know that we need to finish the interview."

My heart sank with an aching slowness with the realization that I'd wanted to help them very badly. "Yes, of course," I said and glanced down. "I'll let the agency know to find another applicant as soon as possible."

But when I moved to step around him, he cupped my elbow. And when I looked up, I was met with smiling eyes.

"What I meant to say was, when can you start?"

I blinked, stunned.

The smile blew out of him just like that. "I mean, if you want. But of course you don't want to. I can't imagine why you would, if I think about it. I shouldn't have asked. This is too much, even for me, and I'm their father," he rambled, punctuating the end of his speech by raking his long fingers through his blond hair.

I suspected his mind kept going even though his lips were still.

"You'd like to hire me?"

"I can't imagine a more practical interview," he answered frankly.

I looked over the three of their hopeful faces and then back at Katie, whose smile was sweet and encouraging. And I met Charlie's eyes, searching for the warning, for the whisper of menace I'd ignored before, but I found none. Instead, I found something far more precarious, disguised as something innocent.

Naive and hopeful trust.

And, before I could talk any sense into myself, I smiled and said, "How about now?"

Lost Future

CHARLIE

The afternoon had been, for lack of a better word, perfect. Maven sat in the crook of my arm as we headed up the stairs after dinner. Hannah followed with Sammy as he hopped up the steps, saying, *Boing, boing, boing*, on a loop. And I was struck with a sense of relief I hadn't felt in what seemed like an age.

Hannah fit in easily, stepping into her role with effortless grace, like she'd been there all along rather than being a complete stranger. The kids were enthralled with her. Sammy had exuberantly dragged her around, asking her to translate things into Dutch, and Maven had clung to her, quiet and content as she was but with more persistence than she usually had with new people.

It was comforting—not only to have help with the kids again, but to have such capable help.

God knew I was unqualified to do it myself. Years without enough practice had left me helpless when my wife left, and I'd been trying to make up ground ever since.

I stopped outside the bathroom and turned to Hannah, who smiled. I smiled back out of instinct.

Sammy bolted into the bathroom and started tugging his shirt off.

Hannah chuckled, watching after him. "Should I go get their clothes or start the bath?"

"Um, I don't know. Maybe you should ..." I stammered, unable to answer even such a simple question. It was rare that I did this, and when I did, it was typically chaos.

But the expression on her face made me feel like it was all okay. "How about I start the bath and you can get their clothes? I'm not sure where their things are."

"Good idea," I said as I set Maven down, thankful for the instruction and an out.

I headed to Maven's room, feeling like a fool. *Come on, Charlie. You're a smart guy, so stop being such an idiot.*

The scolding bolstered me—until I opened her drawer. Her little clothes were all neatly folded inside, and I dug through them, holding them up to each other to try to find a matching shirt and bottoms, but I couldn't seem to figure out a pair.

Was it the pink top with the orange polka dots and the orange bottoms or the pink ones?

I found a nightgown and almost crowed in relief.

Sammy's was easier — everything was either blue or green.

A few minutes later, I headed back to the bathroom, prepared to show Hannah where the towels and washcloths were. But when I reached the threshold, I found she didn't need me to show her anything at all.

Hannah was leaning over the claw-foot tub's rim with her sleeves pushed up, towels stacked on the counter next to the sink and washcloths in the tub. She was singing sweetly in Dutch, I presumed, making a rubber duck dance in the water. Sammy giggled, Maven clapped, and my chest ached.

It seemed so natural for her, and I wished as I had a thousand times that I could be like that. I wished I could take care of them this way, wished I could navigate the day-to-day of parenthood without feeling inept and overwhelmed instead of second-guessing myself like it was my job.

I stepped into the room and flipped the toilet lid down to take a seat, watching, smiling again, that strange expression that had eluded me for so long.

"Find everything okay?" I asked when she stopped singing.

She glanced over at me with a reassuring smile, lips closed sweetly. "Yes, thank you. What's their normal bedtime routine?"

I scratched the back of my neck. "I, um … I don't really know. They bathe around seven thirty, I think, and are in bed around eight." I paused. "I'm sorry. I'm not much help, am I?"

But she just kept on smiling. I wondered absently if she ever stopped.

"It's all right. I don't think there's really a wrong way, is there?"

"No, I suppose there isn't."

She poured baby shampoo into her hand and massaged it into Maven's hair until it was thick with suds. "How about we brush our teeth and read a story?"

Sammy lit up and bounced, sloshing the water around. "Let's read *Pete the Cat!* That's my *faaavorite*!"

She laughed. "Yes, of course."

Satisfied, he picked up a toy boat and motored it in circles, making engine noises with his mouth as Hannah watched him, and I watched her.

I wanted to speak, wanted to make small talk, but I realized I didn't quite know how to anymore. I'd sequestered myself after my wife left, throwing myself into work. Because of the split, I'd lost my friends, lost the life I'd known, and I'd dived into work to try to escape the fact.

"How long have you been in America?" I asked, the most banal of conversational tools in my arsenal.

"Only a few months."

Hannah reached for a plastic cup on the ledge under the frosted window and dipped it in the water, tipping Maven's chin to rinse her hair without getting soap in her eyes. I made note of the trick.

"And you came here to nanny?"

She nodded and shifted to wash Sammy's hair. "I've always loved children, and my best friend has been here as an au pair for two years now. She's been begging me to come here since she stepped off the plane."

"Why'd you leave your last job?" I asked, surprised when she stiffened, her hand pausing for only a split second. "I'm sorry. I don't mean to pry."

"No, it's fine," she reassured, her discomfort gone as quickly as it had appeared. "It's a perfectly reasonable question for my employer to ask. It wasn't quite a good fit. My interview was done over video chat—we secure our employment before we move—so it wasn't as easy to determine how it would be every day, living with a family."

It was a very professional answer, but I couldn't shake the sense that there was more to it. "And you feel like this is a good fit for you?"

"I do," she answered without hesitation as she kneaded Sammy's hair with her long fingers buried in the suds. "I believe you can tell by feeling, an intuition."

"I know what you mean."

She continued, "Interviewing for au pair positions usually takes months, so it was really quite lucky that you needed help so quickly. I'm surprised you went with an au pair agency rather than finding a nanny for that reason."

"I'd actually put in requests with just about every agency in

Manhattan—au pair and nanny alike. I liked the idea of the kids learning another culture, and I missed having someone who lived here. Most nannies aren't willing to make that commitment. My hours are long and late, and it brings me peace of mind, knowing someone isn't waiting for me to get home so they can leave."

"So you did have someone living here? Before your last nanny?" she asked as she rinsed Sammy's hair.

"My ex's sister, Elliot. She lived in your old room for years, ever since Sammy was born."

She didn't speak, the questions hanging in the air, unspoken.

"She left just after Mary, moved on with her life. I almost had to force her to go," I added with a chuckle. "She didn't want to leave me and the kids, but she'd done too much for us already. I hired Jenny, the last nanny, just after Elliot left."

"Well, I'm thankful things worked out and that you offered me the position. Your family is charming, and after staying with a friend for the last few weeks, I'm happy to feel useful again."

"We're happy to have you," I said uselessly.

The conversation lulled, but Hannah didn't seem to mind. She just began humming as she lathered up soap on a washcloth, handing it to Sammy to wash himself, which he did with the gusto only a five-year-old could muster. Then, she lathered up the second cloth, standing Maven up to wash her.

As I watched, I couldn't deny that it felt like a good fit. Even with the chaos that had been in play when she arrived, she had a certain *rightness* about her—in the way she'd stepped in and found her place, like the clicking together of puzzle pieces that set my home in order after a week of upheaval. She had restored a sense of order just in a few hours, which brought me relief and peace that I hadn't felt in a good while, even with our previous nanny.

A few minutes of companionable quiet later, they were rinsed off, and the tub was gurgling as it drained. I stood and unfolded the towels, passing one to Hannah and using the other to dry Sammy off, spending a little too long and a little too much energy on ruffling his hair to make him giggle.

We dressed them and shepherded them into brushing their teeth, and a short while after, Hannah was in Sammy's room, reading him *Pete the Cat,* and I sat in the rocking chair with Maven, reading her a pop-up book about jungle animals, feeling the weight of her in my lap, wondering why I didn't do this more often.

I knew the answer, of course. I'd failed this routine too many times to count, but Hannah had guided me through it just as easily as she had the children. I found myself feeling like maybe I could learn a thing or two. That much, I *did* feel ready for.

I tucked Maven and her stuffed bunny into her white sleigh bed, pulling her pink covers up as she stared at the butterflies and flowers hanging from the high ceiling. I kissed her cheek and told her I loved her, meaning the words from the very depths of my heart.

I closed her door gently and walked down the hall to Sammy's room, leaning on the doorframe to listen as Hannah finished the book. They sat in his captain bed, his room all dark wood and shades of blue with a little bit of a pirate flare—his obsession for a few years now—but the lights were dimmed and dreamy, and the sight hit me in the rib cage.

I owed my children so much more than they'd received, and I vowed as I had so many times that I would find a way to make it up to them.

I only had to figure out how.

An hour later, I'd shown Hannah out, and with her exit, my brain began to whir, recounting the afternoon that had gone so unexpectedly. To say that I was surprised would be the understatement of the century.

That morning, I'd felt nothing but defeat, and as I walked through my foyer and toward the kitchen, I realized that feeling had almost completely passed, leaving me with a calm breath of hope.

I'd opened the door and seen her there, standing on my stoop with the sunlight shining through her long blonde hair framing her face—a small and sweet curve of high cheekbones peppered with freckles, anchored by a narrow chin. Her eyes were blue and big and wide, her lips rosy, smiling, always smiling. And her height had caught me off guard; she was only five or six inches shorter than me—most women maxed out about a foot below my airspace—but she still seemed fragile, delicate, her arms long and slender and waist small.

In the span of a few heartbeats, she'd knocked the rust off me, my gears creaking and groaning to life at the mere sight of her.

I chalked it up to my isolation, to the acknowledgment that I was still a man, a man who had been alone for a long time.

I'd been alone far longer than I'd been single.

I pushed the thought away, considering my children, how I'd been about as helpful as a pair of busted training wheels, wondering what the future held for us. Wondering if I could find a way to what I wanted, wondering if I could even truly define what I wanted. Because my life had been turned upside down and shaken out, leaving a mess I didn't know how to clean up.

I turned the corner into the kitchen where Katie was waiting with a smile.

"Oh, Charlie. She's lovely."

"She really is, isn't she?" I opened the fridge for a beer.

"You sound surprised."

"That's because I am." The door closed with a thunk.

"The kids seem to love her. Hard not to, if you ask me," she baited, watching me with eyes I'd call shrewd if they didn't have the best intentions behind them.

I gave her a knowing look and twisted off the cap.

"Oh, don't gimme that face. I'm just saying, she's awfully young and pretty—on top of being a downright Mary Poppins with the kids."

I took a swig, ignoring the *pretty* part. "I know she's twenty-two but, God, if she doesn't look younger. Or maybe I'm just getting old."

"Never tell an old lady you're old. It smacks of green misunderstanding."

I chuckled, but a sigh slipped out of me at the end. "I didn't quite expect her," I admitted.

"Yes, well, that's how it often goes, isn't it?"

"I suppose."

"What exactly didn't you expect?"

I thought on it for a second. "I don't know. It was just so *easy*. When Jenny started, it took us weeks to find a rhythm, and even then ... well, it just felt like her job, but with Hannah, it feels like her calling. Does that make sense?"

"It does."

"I almost felt like a voyeur, watching her with the kids. It was a lesson in everything I'm doing wrong and a reminder of how much more I could be doing."

"Charlie, no one would ever accuse you of being neglectful. Don't be too hard on yourself," Katie said with chiding softness. "You're doing right by them."

"That's debatable, but thank you all the same." I took another pull of my beer.

"What else?"

"What else what?"

She smirked. "What else didn't you expect?"

"I dunno," I answered noncommittally with a matching shrug.

"For her to be so pretty?"

I rolled my eyes. "You're a mess, Katie."

"True, but you *do* think she's pretty, don't you?"

"I'm a straight man with eyes. Of course I think she's pretty."

Katie laughed, and I took another drink before inspecting the label like it was fascinating.

"Do you think it's bad that I think she's pretty?"

She watched me for a second. "Do *you* think it's bad that you think she's pretty?"

"No, I suppose not. I won't do anything about it, and that's all that matters, right?"

"Sure. But I wouldn't hesitate to befriend her at least. You need somebody beyond your nosy housekeeper to talk to."

I smirked. "I'm that annoying, am I?"

She waved her hand at me. "Hush, that's not what I meant, and you know it."

My smile faded. "Ever since Mary, it hasn't been easy to let people in. You know that—maybe better than anybody."

"I know," she said somberly, her eyes sad. "But that doesn't mean you shouldn't try." She stepped over and rested a hand on my arm. "It's gonna be all right, Charlie. I promise you that."

It was something she'd promised me before, but I didn't believe it any more now than ever.

"Thanks," I said anyway.

"You're welcome." She began untying her apron. "Need anything else from me tonight?"

I shook my head. "Thanks for staying late."

"Oh, it's no trouble. Anything to help the cavalry get settled in and ready to take over the kids. Nothing makes me feel quite as helpless than failing at that particular task."

I knew what she meant far too well to admit aloud. I nodded, but I suspected she gathered my feelings all the same.

Katie left for the night, and I walked through the empty house, pausing at the room that would be occupied by Hannah first thing in the morning. The flooring was dark, the walls too, with a fireplace just opposite her bed. The room felt old, older than the rest of the Victorian house, and I wondered if Hannah would like it, what she would look like there. I imagined her sitting on the bed like a ray of sunshine in the pitch-black of midnight.

With that thought, I pushed off the doorframe and walked back to my office. It was as classic as the rest of the house—with old woodwork and dark floors, the built-in bookshelves framing a window and my desk in front of it, facing the door.

And then I got back to work. Because at least that was something I was good at.

Truth of Circumstance

HANNAH

"Tell me everything," Lysanne said in Dutch as she pulled her pillow into her lap, her face sparking with anticipation and cheeks high as she waited for me to join her.

I laughed and set my bag by the door of her bedroom. "I'll be out of your hair in the morning. I got the job."

She waved her hand at me, and I climbed into her bed and sat across from her.

"Och. I loathe for you to leave, but I'd rather you not be deported. It took me two years to convince you to come here in the first place."

With another laugh, I grabbed a pillow too, mirroring her as we leaned toward each other like little girls.

"How are the children?"

"They're perfectly lovely."

"I can tell by the jam on your sweater. Perfectly lovely."

I glanced down, having forgotten. "I walked into pandemonium. The cook had been watching them, but she couldn't give them the attention they needed and do her job too. They only wanted someone's time, so I gave them mine. It was simple really."

Lysanne shook her head, tucking her long, dark hair behind her ear. "You're the best of us all. I almost killed Sydney today."

I chuckled. "No, you didn't."

She nodded earnestly. "Oh, but I did. She fought me all day about everything—getting dressed, eating lunch, brushing her teeth, taking a bath, going to bed. I practically had to wrestle her into her nightgown as she wailed about not wanting to sleep—they always do that when they're the most tired—and she wouldn't stay in her room, not even for a heartbeat. The moment I left, there she would be, pulling the door back open. I swear, I've never met a more willful six-year-old in all my days."

"All your long, long days in twenty-two years?" I teased.

She rolled her eyes. "Anyway, you likely would have just smiled and sung her a song and not have been bothered at all."

"Oh, you know I can be bothered. You test the limits of that daily."

She laughed and whacked me with her pillow before tucking it back into her lap. "Tell me about the dad," she said, her tone sobering and smile flattening. "He must have been all right if you took the job."

"Yes, I think he's all right." I sighed. "In the moment, it felt right. My instinct said it was safe, that I was safe, that it was a good match. But since the second I left, I've been feeling like I made a mistake. I was hasty to agree without thinking about it, but something about them made me want to say yes. They need my help, and based on what I saw when I walked in, they need my help now. The children are sweet, and Charlie is ... I don't know. Lost, I think. Something in his eyes ... they're the deepest brown, bottomless, sad."

Her brows rose. "*Charlie*, huh? With the bottomless eyes? Yeah, that sounds like there's no danger at all. He's handsome then?"

Another sigh slipped out of me. "Yes, he's handsome. Tall, blond, wealthy, and a single dad." My stomach sank like a stone. "This really is a terrible idea. Do you think … should I refuse? There's still time."

"Well," she started thoughtfully, "you really do need the job, and who knows when another one will come available? This one took weeks. Is he better looking than Quinton?"

At the sound of his name, my heart stopped, starting again with a kick. "I never thought Quinton was handsome."

"Ninety percent of the au pairs we know would have been flat on their backs for him in thirty seconds."

I gave her a look. "Quinton is married. And there are two types of handsome men—the ones who know they're handsome and exploit it whenever possible and the ones who are handsome because they *don't* exploit it. Quinton is the former."

"And Charlie with the bottomless brown eyes is the latter?"

I nodded. "I think so. Plus, the cook told me he's very busy with work and hardly home. When he is, he locks himself in his office. She only had the best and kindest things to say about him, which is another reason I agreed. Quinton treated everyone in the household like property, even the children. They were expected to be seen and not heard, like a pair of matching statues to put on the mantel for display. But Charlie cares very much; it's plain to see on his face, in his body, hear it in his voice."

"And you got all that in an afternoon?"

I shrugged. "It's just a feeling, you know?"

"You've always been that way. I suspect it's why you're so good with children; you have a sixth sense for those kinds of things. I would trust in that. You knew the second you walked into Quinton's house that it was going to end badly."

Goosebumps crept up my arms, and I rubbed my forearm to

warm them away. "I didn't feel anything at all that gave me pause at Charlie's. And I was ready to say no; it was on my lips before he opened the door. But then he opened the door," I said simply, as if it explained everything.

"And if it doesn't work out?" she asked, the look on her face telling me she knew she wouldn't like my answer.

I reached for her hand. "Then it's time I went home. I think we can both admit my coming to America has been a disaster."

She wound her fingers in mine. "I still think you need to give it more of a chance. You've only been here a few months. Don't they say you have to reserve judgment until you've been somewhere for six months?" she asked hopefully.

"Well, most people don't step off the airplane and into a situation like I did. I should have turned around the second I passed the threshold of Quinton's house."

"Maybe this time will be different."

"I hope so. And I hope I can fall in love with this city like you have. I just ... it's not what I thought it would be. Things never are, I suppose, but I didn't expect to feel so ... *separate*. Isolated. I don't belong here, and I don't know if I'll ever feel like I do. And, if things don't work out with this position, I'll go home and not be sad about it, outside of missing you."

She looked worried, so I squeezed her hand and smiled.

"Don't worry about me. Worry about Sydney. I suspect she's in bed, plotting on ways to ruin your day tomorrow."

Lysanne laughed. "Oh, I'm certain of that, the little shrew. Fortunately for her, she's adorable."

I leaned over and pressed my cheek to hers. "I say that about you every day."

I climbed out of bed to get ready for sleep, my mind busying itself with musings of the day to come, the weeks to come, the hopes and fears and uncertainty.

And when the lights were out and sleep crept in, so did the truth of my situation. It was far more dangerous than I'd admitted to myself. But that truth slipped into the sand of slumber, and when I woke, it was hidden away and forgotten, waiting for the wind to uncover it again.

If Only

HANNAH

The next morning when I knocked on the Parkers' door, I was notably less nervous, and when it opened, the scene was noticeably less chaotic.

But Charlie's smile was still as dazzling as it had been the few times I saw it the day before.

"Morning," he said as he grabbed one of my suitcases, then the other.

"Good morning. Thank you."

I stepped in, and he closed the door behind me.

"No problem. I really appreciate you starting so soon." He rolled the suitcases toward the staircase to the lower floor and what would be my bedroom. "I've got to get back to work tomorrow—today really. It's waiting impatiently for me in my office."

I followed. "It's no trouble. The timing worked out nicely."

"That, it did."

We said nothing else as we made our way down the stairs, down the hall, and he turned the corner into my room with my bags.

I stopped outside of the threshold on instinct, warning triggering nerves in a chain up my back at the sight of Charlie in my room. I couldn't force myself in, and I didn't want to.

Calm down. He's safe.

He brought the suitcases to a stop next to a wardrobe and turned to me, his face soft and open, eyes deep and honest though tight in the corners with pain or sadness or regret—I couldn't be sure which. Nothing about him inspired fear, but I stayed put all the same.

"The kids are somehow miraculously asleep, but if they sleep much past nine, it might be hard to get them to nap. I'll be in my office if you need anything that Katie can't help you with."

"Does she work every day?" I asked.

"Sundays are usually her day off, but she's sticking around to help get you settled. She knows far more than I do about running the house," he said with a deprecating chuckle as he started for the door.

My pulse ticked a notch faster with his every step, and I moved out of the way, giving him a wide berth to pass. He paused, watching me curiously, his hand moving as if he might try to touch me, but it fell back to his side.

"We're glad you're here, Hannah," he said softly.

"I'm glad to be here," I said equally soft.

With that, he nodded once and turned for his office, taking my breath with him in a whoosh.

He won't hurt you. You can trust him. You should try.

And I wanted to. He'd done nothing but respect my space, never hinting that he was anything but innocuous. But Quinton's face flashed in my mind, straightening my back, clearing my thoughts.

The differences between Charlie and Quinton struck me, the juxtaposition of emotions they invoked stark. Where Charlie gave me no tangible reason to be concerned, Quinton had made me uncomfortable from the first moment I met him. Something about the way his eyes would linger or the way his handsome lips curled when he smiled.

It wasn't long after I'd moved in that he grew bolder. He would appear in the doorway of the kitchen late at night when I was making tea or make it a point to meet me in the hallway, as if he'd been waiting for a moment to be alone with me in a quiet, unavoidable space.

I'd told myself it was innocent enough, ignoring the warning signs I should have heeded.

Once, he'd touched my hand when his wife had her back turned to us, the feeling of his skin on mine like hot grease.

Once, he'd cupped the curve of my behind and squeezed, his hand disappearing so quickly, I wondered if it had been imagined.

Once, he'd come into the bathroom while I was showering and kindly reminded me to lock it. I had; I'd locked it tight and double-checked it.

Once, he'd come into my room in the dark of night and woken me with his hand up my nightgown and lips against mine.

I'd pushed him away, gotten out of bed, poised to run or scream or fight, and when I'd told him to leave, he had.

I had known it wouldn't be the end. The desire in his eyes had been anchored by an unspoken promise to wait, not to stop. But he'd left my room, and I'd moved the chair in front of the door with shaking hands before packing my bag.

In the morning before I'd left, I'd told him and his wife I had a family emergency and would be leaving immediately for Holland. She'd hugged me and thanked me and wished me well while he watched us embrace with smoldering anger, the sullen, bitter look of one who had lost their toy.

Lysanne's host family had welcomed me, and for two weeks, I'd repaid them with my time while I worked with the agency to place me in a new position. A better position.

And I believed I'd found one. This time, there were no predatory glances, not even a hint of anything but respect. It had been too soon to make the decision to stay, especially since I'd been wrong before. But where Quinton had always felt dangerous, Charlie only felt safe.

Quinton was beautiful in the way a panther was—too strong and sleek and hungry to trust.

Charlie was beautiful in the way a prince was—too noble and honest and virtuous to deny.

To pretend like he wasn't would be a lie and an absolute farce. But it didn't *mean* anything that I saw it and felt it. I'd seen plenty of handsome men, even dated handsome men. I told myself I was just more aware because we'd be living together. And because he wasn't married. And because seeing him with his children did something to me that I couldn't quite describe, awoke some instinctive desire for *that*. Not *him*, but *that*.

The fact that I felt anything at all, even a passing thought of anything past professional interest, should've had me packing, not unpacking as I was, folding my clothes and organizing them in the big wardrobe. But as much as I'd learned, I was still naive, telling myself I was in control. I reminded myself that anyone would be interested in a beautiful, successful single father. Something about the loneliness and determination it took to do something like that inspired respect and an air of allure. It was strictly circumstance, not the man himself. I didn't even know him.

I thought I would do well to keep it that way.

So, I tucked my thoughts away with my sweaters and socks with the hopes they'd stay put.

The room where I stood was old and dark and cozy, the beautiful antique mantel almost imposing but still quaint. It reminded me so much of Holland in that way, a familiarity that touched me with a deep sense of longing. But home wasn't going anywhere. This room was mine only for a time.

Of course, that was sad in its own right, a reminder of how quickly things could change.

By the time I finished unpacking, it was after nine, so I made my way up to the kids' rooms to wake them.

First, Maven, bleary-eyed and sluggish. She hung on me like a koala, and I took a seat in her rocking chair, singing to her for a few minutes as she shook off sleep. The weight of her resting on my chest was a warm comfort, her blonde curls silky in my fingertips as I rocked and hummed and sang. And then she sat, peering at me with the biggest, deepest brown eyes, thumb in her mouth as she touched my cheek with her other hand.

I kissed her cheek and picked her up, heading to Sammy's room.

The moment I whispered, "Good morning," he shot out of bed like a bolt, bright-eyed and asking questions about the day.

"Let's start with breakfast, shall we?" I asked on a laugh.

He agreed with a whoop as he ran out of his room and down the stairs.

When I reached the kitchen, he was already sitting at the table with a muffin on a plate, eating the top of it.

"Mornin'," Katie sang.

"Good morning."

I sat Maven in her booster seat, and Katie appeared at my elbow with a muffin and a cup of milk for her. Maven delicately picked it up and took a small bite.

"And how are you this morning?" Katie asked, making her way back over to the island where she'd laid out a spread for me.

"Quite well, thank you. How early do you get here most days?"

She shrugged. "About six, give or take. Later on Saturdays."

I loaded a plate with fruit and a croissant. "I'm sorry you had to come in today."

She waved me off. "Oh, it's fine. I'm glad to help out, even gladder that you're here and I can go back to single duty instead of double. Not that I don't love the angels, but I'd rather be scrubbing baseboards on my knobby old knees than trying to keep them out of trouble. I have a hard enough time keeping *myself* out of trouble."

I laughed and took a seat at the bar. "Does their mother not live in town to help?"

Katie's lips flattened out. "Oh, she does. She works just up Amsterdam, at Mount Sinai."

My face quirked in confusion.

She didn't wait for me to ask; the question must have been plain on my face. Her voice lowered. "She's abandoned all of them—her whole life outside of her job. She hasn't seen the children since she left last winter."

I found I had nothing to say and no appetite for my breakfast. I watched Maven eating her muffin with methodical gentility, wondering how in the world their mother could leave have left them so easily.

But I caught myself. I didn't know her, couldn't possibly know how difficult or easy it had been. Perhaps guilt had been slowly eating away at her. Maybe she'd tried to come back. Maybe she didn't believe herself fit.

The thought made me feel better than the image of her as a monster. So, I clung to that.

"Do they miss her?" I asked, glancing at Sammy, who was humming and so intent on his breakfast, he didn't seem to be listening at all.

"Hard to say. I've never heard them mention her."

"How strange," I muttered.

But Katie chuffed. "Not really. Word is, she wasn't winning any awards for Mother of the Year. Wife of the Year either." She leaned forward even more, her voice almost a whisper. "She cheated on Charlie. It went on for years right under his nose—and with his best friend."

A slow tingle worked down my spine. "Oh my God."

Katie nodded, her shoulders rising and falling with a sigh. "He lost all his friends. Seemed they'd all known about the affair and failed to tell him. And Mary left the house straightaway, nearly disappeared. His parents came for a bit while he secured me and Jenny and got us all set up." She shook her head. "Charlie was a mess in those days. But that's a story for another time." Her eyes shifted to the entrance to the kitchen, and she straightened up. "Tea or coffee?" she asked, turning the conversation with the question.

"Tea would be lovely, thank you." I answered.

She nodded and turned on the kettle. I watched the kids eat their breakfast, wondering over how it had all come about, how he had handled it all, how he'd felt and what he'd been through.

I sighed. I could wonder all day long, but there was no way for me to understand just how badly he'd been hurt. The errant thought that he might have been to blame crossed my mind, but I couldn't truly convince myself, not after what I'd seen, however brief the glimpses I'd gotten were. He'd have to be a spectacular actor to walk around with the weight on his shoulders and the sadness in his eyes, to pretend to love his children. You couldn't manifest love where there was none. It was no easier than stopping it once it took hold.

I always believed evil could be seen, sometimes in the smallest, quietest places. But those quiet places were also where you could see courage, strength, goodness.

Charlie had only shown me the latter, and Katie had confirmed my belief that he would have tried to do the right thing. And I clung to that more tightly than I probably should.

CHARLIE

I shouldn't have locked myself in my office all day, but I did.

It had been innocent. I always worked on Saturdays, sometimes from home, but I'd taken the day before off to acclimate Hannah, which had left me with some catching up to do. I'd lost myself in the task at hand, and before I knew how late it had gotten, Katie popped her head in to say goodbye for the day.

I'd taken both lunch and dinner at my desk, and by the time Hannah came in to let me know the kids were long asleep and that she was turning in, I remembered something very vital.

My wishes for wanting more time to spend with my children were futile.

I tried to tell myself that maybe, if I could get on top of my workload, I could find a way to come home early a few days a week. I could take a few hours off on the weekends for dinner or lunch or bedtime. But that was a lie of its own. There was no getting on top of things. The onslaught of things to do never ceased, never slowed, and even if I found some way to catch up, I'd never get ahead.

Instead, I'd only have more work to pile on.

With Hannah's presence came the desire to hide myself away, to be alone. It was a new person in my space after a long, long while with things being the same. It felt like an intrusion. Not to say it was unpleasant, just foreign, distracting.

It was a reminder of just how alone I'd been—that something so simple as a new nanny would affect me beyond the obvious.

There were times when I missed my old life, missed the days of drinks and dinners and outings with friends, missed the days when I'd had less work and more time. When I'd gotten on my feet after

Mary left, I'd thrown myself into work so completely that, after a few months, I'd earned a promotion—a promotion that increased my workload by a large enough margin to consume any free time I'd enjoyed. And, until recently, the distraction had been welcome.

But I missed the camaraderie of friends, the comfort of a relationship, even if it was all wrong, even if it wasn't real.

Being alone, I'd found, was easier in too many ways to risk venturing back out into the land of the living. At least this way, I couldn't get hurt again.

This house, every room, everything inside—including the three beating hearts—was colored with lost memories and wishes blown to the wind, never to come true.

When I'd met Mary, I had been studying for the bar exam, and she had just started her residency. We'd had precious little free time, but in that free time, we had been together, blowing off steam. And I'd liked her well enough.

How was that for a declaration? *She's pretty okay.*

At the time, I hadn't been thinking past the weekend.

And then she'd told me she was pregnant.

She'd broken the news with tears and anger, and I'd held her and promised her it would be all right. The trouble was that I had been stupid enough to think it would be. I'd convinced myself that our commonalities could translate to love.

There had been no way of knowing at the time that she wasn't capable of giving her love, not to me, not to anyone. And I hadn't realized it until Sammy was born. Day by day, little by little, my hope had chipped away until it changed into a twisted, broken version of the original, and I'd covered my eyes and pretended like it was all just fine. Just fine. It would work out. My beautiful life was just around the corner.

What I wanted had *always* been just around the corner, and I'd been chasing it, turn after turn, trying to catch it. Sometimes, I'd catch a glimpse before it was gone, giving me false hope that I might be gaining.

But in the end, I was always a little too late.

I had been fortunate in a lot of ways. My parents had planned well enough to pay for my college outright and were wealthy enough to help us with the down payment on the house. My job at the firm had paid more than enough to support us, and with Mary's income included, we had done very well. Better than well.

But money wasn't enough to make us happy, and kids weren't enough to keep us together. Neither of those statements would surprise anyone in the world but me and her.

The end hadn't been kind to either of us. Endings never were.

I'd spent years pretending like things were fine. We'd survived only by working as many hours as we could just to keep ourselves occupied. Of course, Mary had kept herself occupied in other ways, too. Like in my best friend's bed. For two years.

She'd lied, lied to me, lied to herself. She'd betrayed us all, and her only regret was that I'd found out. I knew this because I had known her as best as anyone could, as one would silently observe a snake from behind glass. She had been interested in self-preservation, nothing more—not from me, not from him—and we'd both learned it far too late.

When I'd learned what she'd done, I should have been lost. When she'd disappeared into thin air, I should have been split open. I should have felt the sting of loss like a quick blade when I held my crying son and told him I didn't know where she was. When I'd stood in my room and stared at her open dresser, her clothes hanging from the drawers in hasty, spewing stillness, I should have felt *something*.

But I hadn't.

It was where I'd been ever since—a gray wasteland where every day was the same. There was no color, no spark, no life. Just work and failed fatherhood and sleeping and eating and working in a Sisyphean loop without a goal or end.

My phone messages asking her how she wanted to handle custody had gone unanswered. My emails with rundowns of our options were never returned. My efforts to try to get things moving had been met with silence.

I'd tried to give her time. Maybe she was as broken down as I had been those first few months after she left. I'd wanted to believe she'd come around. And it wasn't until I had been desperate for a resolution that I went to Mount Sinai where she worked.

I remembered walking off the elevator, seeing her from behind, her head bent as she'd jotted in a file, hair in a tight ponytail, blue scrubs and lab coat as nondescript as any of the other doctors that passed. But I had known it was her, known it as well as I knew my own hands and as distantly as I knew my own children. She was a part of me, and she was alien—foreign and familiar. I knew her, and I had no idea who she was.

She turned and saw me, her face caught in some mix of emotions—fear, pain, failure, dismay. And then her lips flattened, her eyes closing her off behind an iron wall.

As if I were to blame. As if I had left her. As if I'd done anything but honored my promise to her even though I knew deep down in the quiet places of my heart that she didn't love me.

As if I had slept with *her* best friend.

Former best friend.

But even Jack hadn't kept her. He'd realized what I'd known all along—Mary was too selfish to ever love anyone but herself.

Once she'd processed me standing before her, she'd turned on her heel and hurried away, ignoring me as I chased her through the hall, easily dodging me by ducking into a corridor for hospital staff that required a key entry. And I'd stood outside of that door for a long while, staring through the small square panes of glass, wondering how I'd found myself in that place, in that moment.

I'd been trying to get her to work with me, to negotiate, and I had only been met with silence. That day was the final straw. She didn't care, and she never would. So, I'd filed for divorce without her, and I had given her no quarter with my terms.

But she'd only ignored that, too. The divorce papers had gone unsigned, and the temporary custody hearing had gone on without her, her seat cold and empty. And I'd found myself alone, except not alone. I had my kids to care for. Everything had fallen on me, and I'd had no idea how to handle it all.

So, I didn't. I couldn't.

I'd like to blame my job for my failures. Working eighty-plus hours a week at a law firm didn't lend a lot of time for anything besides sleeping and eating, and even those were sometimes luxuries. I'd like to blame Mary for not being my partner or for her inability to love even her own children.

It was a cruel thing to think, and I supposed I didn't really mean it. I believed, somewhere in her, she cared. It was only that those feelings were buried under so many layers of self-importance that not only could she not find them, but she had no desire to.

And so I'd decided to learn to be a father, to learn how to give my children the love they hadn't gotten from either of us. What I hadn't counted on was my absolute ineptitude.

I was too broken and afraid to step in, in the way they deserved.

In all those years of hiding away from my marriage, I'd hidden from them, too. And I'd been away so long, I couldn't find my way back to them, the path grown over and wild and gone. And I was lost somewhere inside the tangle.

By the time I finally came out of the office, the house was dark and silent with sleep. Moonlight was the only light in my room as I moved to the closet and peeled off my clothes. The nightlight was the only light in the bathroom, and I didn't change that either as I brushed my teeth, watching my reflection.

I looked older than I should and younger than I felt.

The last nine months had taken a toll on me. I supposed deep down I knew the pace of my life wasn't sustainable, that if I kept going as I was, I'd crash and burn and take everything down with me.

Honestly, I was surprised I hadn't already.

But I couldn't find a way out of the cycle. I'd broken the bone that controlled my speed, and my life had kept careening forward as I hung on and closed my eyes and hoped that what sped up would someday slow down. Part of the problem was that I hadn't questioned it nearly enough.

But after yesterday and the introduction of Hannah into our lives, I found myself considering it much more earnestly. Her energy had me blown off course, just a step, just enough to make me crack my eyes and take a look at where I was, and I didn't like what I saw.

And as I climbed between my sheets, I tried to close my eyes again, tried to force them shut, tried to find peace.

But it was no use.

Firelight

CHARLIE

For a full week, I did little besides work in an effort to gain a little ground, fueled by the desire to earn myself time off.

I hadn't seen Hannah much, mostly just in the mornings on my way out. But last night, I'd come home from work early enough to eat with the kids before sojourning in my office to burn the midnight oil.

And it had felt good.

I'd even helped out a little at bedtime, the task made simple with Hannah at my elbow, offering comfort and a smile that gave me confidence.

Of course, Hannah was always smiling, and I always found myself smiling back. It was a foreign feeling, something so natural, but my face almost resisted it, as if those muscles had atrophied from disuse.

There was just something about that simple curve of her lips, so wide and honest. I didn't know her very well, but that smile made me feel like I did.

Off to work I would go every day, too busy to consider much of anything—not my failures or shortcomings or the beautiful, young au pair who had moved in with me. At least I had a plan, and that plan required me to work, stay on top of my shit, and earn myself some time.

Of course, then a new merger landed on my desk, and what little ground I'd gained was lost just like that.

The buying and selling of businesses wasn't a process that slept, not even when the lawyers did. Instead, the work piled up, the contracts that needed revisions stacked in a never-ending pylon of legal speak and clauses and subclauses and addendums.

It was a brutal business—mergers and acquisitions. We were wheelers and dealers, loophole finders and corner trimmers, dotters of *I*s and crossers of *T*s.

And I hated it.

It was soul-sucking and draining. I'd been at my firm—a big-shot firm with a reputation for working with predatory efficiency—for six years, and it was too late to switch gears, too late to change the course any quicker than the Titanic could have when that poor sap had rung the iceberg alarm.

It was a quandary I'd considered a lot over the nine months since Mary left. Don't get me wrong; I'd contemplated *every* decision I'd made since I first agreed to go out with her. But my career was the only one I felt I could maybe *do* something about.

What that something was, I had no clue. All I knew was that, with every year and month and week that had passed, I'd been finding myself less and less enchanted by the money or the toll it took on me.

I sighed and picked up my highlighter that Saturday afternoon, bowing my head over the contract in front of me with my goal pushed to the forefront of my mind and my regrets pushed back.

A small knock rapped on the door.

"Come in," I said distantly, eyes still on the page, expecting Katie with food, judging by the state of my empty stomach.

"Hello. Katie sent me with your lunch."

My eyes snapped up at the first syllable from Hannah's lips. She walked toward me with a tray of food and a quiet smile.

I set my highlighter down and moved the papers aside, standing to greet her, instantly aware of her presence.

Sly, Katie. Real sly.

"Thanks, Hannah. I'm sorry."

"Whatever for?" she asked as I took the tray.

"For serving me, I guess. I don't expect you to wait on me." I fumbled a little, feeling sheepish.

"Oh, it's all right. I don't mind. The children are just down for their nap."

"Good." I stood there stupidly in the middle of the room, tray in my hands, uncertain of what to say.

She nodded once and shifted as if to leave, the smile still playing at her lips.

"So, how are you liking it so far?" I asked a little too loudly.

"I like it very much, thank you. The children are lovely. We made pasta necklaces this morning. Sammy made you one, too, with wagon wheels. He said you were a cowboy."

I set the tray on my desk before sitting on the edge of it. "I only play one on TV."

Hannah laughed, and I found myself relaxing, feeling at ease, feeling comfortable.

"Katie's wonderful, too. She's made me feel very much at home."

"She does that. It's a wonder how I ever survived without her. My parents were here for a while after my wife left, and it was hard to let them go back home. The only thing that made it easier was Katie. She's almost like family. Like a well-meaning, meddling, loving aunt who makes a mean roast."

A little chuckle passed her lips, but she didn't offer a response.

"Your room is okay?" I asked, the urge to keep the conversation going nudging me on.

"It's just fine. I wondered ... does the fireplace work?"

"It does. We've got wood around back. I'll show you where it is and how to tend it, if you'd like."

"Oh, that's all right. I'm sure I can sort it out, thank you."

So polite. Demure almost.

The conversation lulled again, the silence strained, though we were both smiling. She didn't seem to want to leave any more than I wanted her to.

The realization surprised me, the desire for her company shocking and mildly inappropriate.

Dangerous, Charlie. Let her go. She's your nanny.

Oh, but if she weren't, some quiet part of my mind whispered.

I cleared my throat and stood. "Let me know if you change your mind about the fireplace. And thank you for lunch."

"You're welcome," she said and left the room, closing the door with a snick.

I sighed again, this one heavier than before. God, she was gentle, soft, so different from what I'd known.

Mary had been anything but soft, anything but warm. And Hannah was the absolute opposite, even down to their appearance; where Hannah was fair and colored like spring and sunshine, Mary had dark hair and dark eyes and porcelain skin, like winter branches against cold white snow.

But it didn't matter how different Hannah was or how welcome that difference was. It didn't matter for so many reasons, reasons that began and ended with Hannah's role in my home.

She was my nanny and nothing more.

The day wore on, though I didn't see Hannah again. Katie came for the empty tray with a slick smile but said nothing, and neither did I. Next thing I knew, Katie returned with a dinner tray.

I'd barely made a dent in work.

The sun had gone down by the time I finally had enough, my brain sputtering and mixing up words in its exhaustion. No amount of stretching could ease my stiff, aching back, but I tried anyway.

With a sigh, I stood, perking up when I opened the door and smelled something baking, something sweet. I followed my nose and the sound of laughter, stopping just outside the kitchen.

Hannah stood at the island, and my children sat on the surface, around a mixing bowl. Lemons and blueberries were scattered around the egg crate, oil, and a brand-new bag of flour—brave of her, I'd say.

Maven's face was purple from blueberries; one rested between her thumb and forefinger, and she placed it into her mouth with grace—for a three-year-old. Sammy was singing a song that repeated the word *lemonberry* at varying heights and decibels, and Maven was dancing, a bouncing sort of head-bobbing motion. And Hannah was stirring the batter, smiling down into the bowl, occasionally meeting Sammy's eyes to bob her head in solidarity of his musical endeavor.

The room wasn't overly bright, the dimmers turned down about halfway, painting the room in golds and browns and softness. Katie was nowhere to be seen.

The timer on the oven went off, and Hannah wiped her hands on her apron, reaching for a pot holder before opening the stove and pulling out a pan of muffins. Sammy cheered, and Maven dipped her finger in the batter, looking at Sammy to be sure he hadn't seen her. He hadn't.

When Hannah set the muffins down and turned, when she caught my eye, her face lit up with a smile that hit me in places long left sleeping. I smiled back and stepped into the room, feeling light and heart-full at the same time, my exhaustion swept away by the scene in the kitchen, leaving me feeling calm and peaceful and *good*.

"It smells incredible in here," I said.

"We're making *ka-varker-tarts*!" Sammy crowed.

Hannah laughed. *"Kwarktaarts."*

"That's what I said! *Ka-vark-tarts*!"

Another laugh. "Yes, of course. And what do you call these?" She held up a blueberry.

His face screwed up in concentration. *"Bosbes?"*

"Well done!" she cheered and ruffled his hair. "You'll be speaking Dutch in no time."

I wandered over to the muffins, salivating. "Blueberry muffins?"

She tilted her head from side to side. "Sort of. It's lemon-blueberry quark cake. Well, these are muffins. We're still working on the cake."

I picked one up, hot or not. It smelled too good not to.

"Be careful," she said with a laugh.

"Please, step back, ma'am. I'm a trained professional." I bounced the muffin between my hands, unwrapping it as I went while my salivary glands worked overtime. Once it was free, I broke off a steaming piece, held it as long as I had the patience for, and popped it in my mouth.

Where it promptly melted.

I thought I saw my brain when my eyes rolled back in my head, and a low moan rumbled up my throat. "Oh my God," I said in the second between swallowing and shoving another bite in.

She leaned against the island counter, watching me eat with an amused look on her face and her arms wound around her small waist.

"No fair, Daddy! I want one too," Sammy said with a magnificent pout.

"Sorry, son. These are all mine." I pretended to gobble them all, and he squealed my name.

When I turned around, I popped the rest of heaven in my mouth. I peeled the wrapper from another muffin and broke it in half to blow on it. When the steam was mostly wafted off, I offered half to Sammy and the other half to blueberry-faced Maven.

They greedily tucked in, and I reached for another muffin, practically drooling still as I hurried to unwrap it.

"God, Hannah, what'd you put in this? Crack?"

"What's crack?" Sammy asked with his mouth full.

"A special kind of sugar," I answered around a bite.

Hannah laughed again, grazing her lips with her knuckles. "The secret is the cheese."

I warily eyed the muffin. "There's cheese in here?"

She nodded. "That's what makes it so moist."

I shrugged and shoved another bite down the hatch. "It's unreal, Hannah."

"Thank you," she said, turning back to her bowl to pour the batter into a Bundt pan. "All right, who's going to help me with the *bosbes*?"

"Me!" Sammy cheered, raising his hand while Maven clapped.

She offered them a dish of berries. "All right, just like last time. Put them on the top very gently, like this." She demonstrated, placing a few blueberries on top of the batter.

The kids followed suit.

I unwrapped another muffin. "Gee, Hannah, I'm not sure how having you around will work out for my waistline."

She smiled at me over her shoulder. "Oh, I think you'll be all right."

Hannah hadn't said a single salacious thing, but I couldn't help feeling like there was some underlying meaning to her words. Maybe it was something in her voice, the hint of softness, or maybe it was the way she looked at me, like I meant something, like I was special. It made me feel like *more*, made me wish I were more.

Maybe I was high off her crack cakes.

More likely, I was just stupid.

"Do all the Dutch bake this well?" I asked, eager to halt the train of thought I'd found myself riding.

"I'm sure quite a few do. My grandfather owned a bakery, and my grandmother, mother, and aunt ran it after he died. Baking has just always been in the family, I suppose."

"Do you enjoy it?" I asked as I took another bite, slowing down.

When she turned with the pan, her cheeks were high and rosy. "Oh, I love it. To take bits of things and turn them into something whole, something more. The time and care that goes into making something that brings someone else pleasure. The routine of it—measuring, stirring, kneading. The smells and the warmth of the oven … all of it. I love it."

"Think you'll take over the business?"

"No. My eldest sister and eldest cousin have taken over in our mothers' places." She sounded a little sad, and the thought that she couldn't have what she wanted sent a bolt of irrational anger through me.

I frowned. "Well, that's not fair."

She opened the oven and met my eyes as she slid the pan in. "You sound like Sammy," she teased.

"The kid's got a point."

"It would be nice, but I'm happy. And I'll find a job that makes me happy. I'm sure of that." She set the timer.

"Hannah, can we have cake tonight too?" Sammy asked.

She used her towel to wipe off his hands before dusting his nose. "Not tonight. It won't be cool and ready to eat until you're far away in dreamland." She lifted him off the counter and set him down, picking up Maven. "Come, come. Let's go take a bath, yeah?"

Sammy cheered, and Maven clapped again.

Hannah was still smiling when she looked back at me. "I'll be back to clean up, okay?"

I nodded, feeling like I should step in, take over. But in the end, I just said, "Thanks, Hannah," and watched her disappear.

The moment I was alone in the quiet kitchen, I was struck by a realization. I wasn't miserable. For a minute, I wasn't tired or angry or remorseful. I'd almost call it happy.

The moments had been so few and far between, and they always seemed to come with a price. Playing with the kids made me feel ashamed for not playing with them more. Talking with Katie reminded me of how alone I was. It was always something.

For a minute, for a little sliver of time, I felt like my old self, the old version of me who had thought he was happy, who had felt like he was enjoying life, who'd joked and laughed, and who hadn't felt like scum, even if I was. I might have been in denial back then, but at least I'd found some semblance of joy in my life. The sight of my children happily helping Hannah bake, topped with Hannah's easy smile and peaceful presence, made me forget all about the rest.

Of course, I still let Hannah take the kids upstairs, momentarily paralyzed by doubt in my abilities, the product of months of avoiding my responsibilities out of fear and guilt, which only made the guilt worse and the fear stronger. The cycle I found myself in was vicious, and I wanted out. I just had to figure out *how* to get out.

With a sigh, I looked around the mess in the kitchen. I might be a coward, but I was still a gentleman, goddammit. And so I rolled up my sleeves and got to work.

HANNAH

I gently closed Sammy's door, waving at him until the crack was too small for us to see each other anymore. Maven had gone to sleep easily after a book in the rocking chair, but Sammy had required three books, a drink of water, and a trip to the bathroom before he let me go. I waited a moment longer outside his door, just in case. And, when I was fairly certain he wasn't coming back out, I headed downstairs.

It had been a good day, a fun day, but a tiring one. And it wasn't over, I realized, as I remembered the mess in the kitchen. But when I turned the corner, the kitchen was quiet and spotless.

"Huh." I smiled, hands on my hips.

And then I went in search of Charlie to offer my thanks.

He wasn't in the living room, and a glance upstairs told me he wasn't in his room. So, down the stairs I went to the ground floor, heading for his office. But when I passed my room, I found him in the last place I'd expected, kneeling in front of my fireplace, arranging logs.

The surprise at seeing him in my room, uninvited, sent a shock through me, buzzing over my skin, raising the hair on my arms and the back of my neck.

He smiled when he saw me standing in the hall outside the doorway, but when he noticed that I was rooted to the spot, drowning in unkind memories, his smile faded.

"Are you okay?" he asked cautiously.

"What are you doing in my room?" I asked, my voice quavering just a little, just enough to betray me.

He heard my fear and bolted to his feet with wide eyes. "God, I'm sorry. I shouldn't have come in here without … you know, without your permission, without asking you. I was just going to bring some wood to your door, but it was open, and I thought … well, I just thought it would be nice for you to come in to a fire since I knew you wanted one, and you've done so much for me. Plus, the flue is a little dodgy, and I just … I should go," he rambled, running his hands through his hair as he started for the door.

But as I looked him over, I knew he meant every word he'd

said. Nothing was written in his body and face and eyes but apology and concern.

I reminded myself that he had no idea about Quinton, who would have advanced on me with single-minded determination, not keeping his distance, like I was an animal set to bolt.

It wasn't so far from the truth.

But I wasn't afraid of Charlie. I was afraid because of Quinton, and the difference between those two sentiments settled into my mind and heart.

I stepped into the room, palms out, voice soft. "No, I'm sorry. That was kind of you to help."

He stopped, looking unsure. "Of course. I'm just … I didn't mean to overstep."

I offered a smile, and he relaxed, smiling back.

"It's all right. Thank you for cleaning up after me, too."

He shrugged and glanced into the fireplace. The light was dim, but I thought he might be a little flushed. "I could say the same. The kids go to bed all right?"

"Just fine."

"Thanks for sending them down to say goodnight. Jenny never did that." Some thought passed behind his eyes but slipped away.

"Of course."

"Let me show you how this works." He waved me over, and I walked to him, kneeling by his side as he lit a log covered in a paper bag. "I use these starter logs because I'm lazy."

I chuckled.

"There's a whole stack of them in the shed with the wood. I'll leave you some matches, but it's pretty straightforward. Put this one on the bottom, stack wood on top, light the starter, and voila." His smile fell when he saw my face. "Wait, do you know how to do this?"

I laughed; I couldn't help it. "I've started a fire or two."

"I bet you have." His voice had a wondrous, velvety sheen on it. When I met his eyes, he looked away with a snap. "Not that it's all that complicated. Anyway, here's how the flue works. It's right here." He showed me a small lever. "Open to the right, closed to the left. But it won't really move unless you jiggle it downward first. Otherwise, it's easy as pie. Or *kwarktaart*."

I laughed again. "Thank you, Charlie."

"You're welcome. I'll bring in some more wood for you tomorrow. That way, you can make a fire whenever you'd like."

He stood, dusting off his hands, and I stood, too. We'd been close when we were kneeling, putting us almost too close, but neither of us stepped back, leaving us just inside of what should be comfortable. It was enough of an invasion that my nerves triggered in succession down my back and arms to the tips of my fingers—not with warning or danger, but unexpected desire.

A moment hung between us, just a few heartbeats with our eyes on each other.

And then he looked away.

I took a step back, embarrassed and confused.

"I'll ... ah," he stammered. "All right. Well, um, sleep well. I'll see you in the morning."

"Goodnight" My cheeks blazed, and I was thankful the room was fairly dark.

He nodded, and I thought he might be blushing too as he stepped around me.

I watched him go and let out a breath.

He didn't go upstairs but back into his office. I heard the door close down the hall. The thought that he was still so close made me anxious, made me wonder, sent the questions zipping around my head like hummingbirds. He hadn't intended for ... whatever that was to happen. He'd honestly been trying to be thoughtful, and he was. He was thoughtful and handsome and charming, and he wasn't Quinton.

And I'd wanted him to kiss me. For one brief, careless moment, I'd thought he would, wished he would.

That admission left me reeling.

So I closed and locked the door and changed my clothes, slipping in bed with a book to set my mind to rights while the fire crackled, hoping to turn my thoughts to anything besides the man sitting on the other side of my wall.

So Simple

CHARLIE

The next morning, I was up and in my office before anyone was awake, attacking my work with newfound enthusiasm and a plan in mind. Because I wanted to feel like I'd felt the night before in the kitchen again, and there was only one way to get that back.

Today, I would take a few breaks and be present. Today, I would change, work be damned. Today would mark the first real attempt. Because change wouldn't happen on its own. I had to *make* it happen. And to make it happen, I would have to put boundaries in place, starting with my weekends.

I checked the clock around eleven that morning and closed my laptop, pushing away from my desk and heading up the stairs in search of my children.

When I rounded the corner into the kitchen, I found them sitting at the table with their lunches. And when they saw me, their smiles validated my grand plans with unwavering certainty.

"Hey, guys," I said, smiling back as I walked over to them, ruffling Sammy's hair when I passed him.

"Hi, Daddy," he said.

Maven's mouth was full, so she just waved, and Hannah smiled at me from the island where she was setting up a spread for sandwiches.

I snagged a grape off Maven's plate and popped it into my mouth. She handed me another, which I accepted.

"Thanks, pumpkin."

"Are you done working?" Sammy asked hopefully.

"'Fraid not, bud. But I thought I'd come have lunch with you. Is that okay?"

"Yeah! Want a Nilla Wafer?"

"Psh, *obviously*. And I thought we could play for a little bit before I have to get back to work. What do you say?"

He nodded, grinning. "We can play trucks! You be the bulldozer and I'll be the tractor and Maven can be the monster truck and Hannah can be the ambulance because she helps people."

"Perfect," I said on a chuckle.

A burst of color caught my eye. A vase on the windowsill behind the table held a spray of red and orange tulips.

"Those are beautiful," I said, gesturing to them. "Where did they come from?"

"Oh, I picked them up this morning," Hannah said with that ever-present smile.

"Feeling homesick?"

"Always a little. But I love having fresh flowers in the house, something bright and delicate and alive. Well, maybe not alive anymore, but it *feels* alive, doesn't it?"

"It does," I said as I moved to her side.

"Can I make you a sandwich?" Hannah asked.

"Nah, I think I can manage, thanks. How's it going this morning?"

"It's good. We went to the park this morning."

"I rode my bike!" Sammy crowed.

"Did you? No bumps or scrapes?"

"Nope!"

"I'm impressed. Maybe next time I can come too," I said, hoping it was something I could deliver as I reached into the bread bag for a stack.

Hannah turned to the cupboard, returning with a plate for me.

"Thank you."

She was still smiling, standing at my side, assembling her sandwich. It was so mundane, something completely and utterly boring, but like the weirdo that I was, I found myself watching her hands as she folded cold cuts. We worked around each other—not that it was complicated, but there was a sort of rhythm between us, a natural pace wherein I used what she wasn't and finished just as she needed what I had. I wasn't sure why I noticed it, but I did, and I appreciated the simple synchronicity of the moment, a breath where things were easy.

I passed her the mustard as she handed me the ham. "So, I was thinking ..." I paused.

"Oh, were you?" She glanced over at me with a hint of mirth at the corners of her lips.

"I know. I almost sprained something."

Hannah laughed gently.

"If it's okay, I think I'd like to try to handle bedtime tonight."

"Of course it's okay; they're your children." That time, her laughter was sweet.

"Do you ... would you ... do you think you could maybe ..."

She shifted to face me, her eyes full of encouragement.

"Would you mind ... helping me?"

Hannah nodded, her smile opening up. "That's what I'm here for.

Just let me know what you'd like me to do."

I smiled back. "I'm sorry. I know it sounds stupid. I just … I haven't done this much on my own, but I'd like to start."

Her eyes softened, caught by slanting light, lighting up with sunshine. "There's nothing to be afraid of," she said simply.

I didn't speak.

"There's no right or wrong, and they don't care about anything other than you being there. It's simple enough; you only have to try."

"Is it really that easy?"

"It really is. You'll see." She reached for my arm and gave it a squeeze that wasn't meant to be anything but friendly but held something *more*, something in the pressure in her fingertips and the depths of her eyes.

It was something I did my very best to ignore. But I felt the heat of those fingertips long after they were gone, even as we sat across the table from each other eating lunch, the tulips in the vase behind her bowing their long heads as the sunlight illuminated them, exposing what was hidden within their petals.

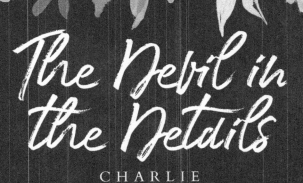

The Devil in the Details

CHARLIE

Over the span of the next two weeks, Hannah taught me more about parenting than I'd learned in five years, and at the heart of it all was the simple truth she had offered. I only had to try.

The kids didn't notice when I fumbled; they only noticed that I was there.

On the weekends when I was home, I would take over bedtime duties with Hannah by my side. I learned how to wash Maven's hair without getting soap in her eyes. I knew how to match their pajamas and what their favorite books were. I even memorized *Where the Wild Things Are* and *Pete the Cat* since Sammy insisted on reading any book three times in a row—at minimum. I knew their favorite toys to sleep with and how long it would take to rock Maven before she fell asleep.

It was a wealth of knowledge that made me feel rich and full and satisfied.

My old nanny hadn't cared like Hannah did. Don't get me wrong; Jenny had loved the kids but in a no-nonsense way. But it just seemed to be in Hannah's nature to love freely and easily.

The thought sent a fresh flash of guilt through me. Because my wife hadn't even been able to care, not like Hannah did.

Our children had been an inconvenience to her, too loud and noisy and demanding for someone such as her. No baths had been given or songs sung, no books read or kisses goodnight. She'd put that on her sister instead.

When I'd imagined my life, my family, my future, I'd imagined something like it had now become and with someone like Hannah. I didn't mean Hannah herself, but the *idea* of her—the idealistic, innate happiness she sparked in my children, in me, in the air.

Before I'd been old enough and experienced enough to know better, I'd turned down a path that led to so much pain and unhappiness. I'd chosen unwisely, and while that union had brought me my children, I'd missed the full extent of what could have been. It underscored my shortcomings, as if the universe wanted me to see all I'd lost and acknowledge it.

I saw it. I saw it, and it was so tangible, so real, it was staggering.

But that pain was balanced by the utter rightness of having Hannah there, of seeing someone, anyone, bring joy into my children's lives, someone to give me peace of mind for their welfare with an instant, satisfying certainty.

And then there was Hannah and *me*.

The night I'd made a fire in her room was the first of many long, drawn out moments, moments I began marking time by over the course of those two weeks. She always seemed to catch me by surprise—the way she smelled, like vanilla and sugar; the blueness of her eyes, speckled with midnight, like a robin's egg; her smile, easy and soft. So many times, I'd found myself close enough to her that I was stunned still and silent, and like a fool, I didn't always pull away.

There were signs of her presence were everywhere. Artwork she'd done with the kids covered my cubicle walls in a riot of color over the drab industrial gray. The vase on the window ledge in the kitchen always held fresh-cut flowers that she'd brought home. That morning, they were pink peonies, their buds still closed. The house always smelled like a bakery now too; she'd taken up baking almost every day when the kids were at school and then with the kids on the weekends. More mouth-watering pastries had come out of my kitchen than in the history of the hundred-twenty-year-old house, I'd be willing to bet.

My environment had changed, and I found I'd changed a little, too. Not enough, but it was a start.

And it felt good.

That morning, I hung my suit coat on the back of a dining chair when I walked into the kitchen where the kids were eating, Hannah between them, all three of them smiling up at me.

Mornings used to be a time for bedlam, but everyone seemed calm and happy and ready for the day, myself included.

"Morning," I said, smiling back at all of them. I'd been doing quite a bit of that lately, too.

Katie handed me a cup of coffee with a wink, and I took a seat on a barstool, facing out toward the table.

"How'd everyone sleep?"

Hannah nodded and wiped yogurt off Maven's face. "Well, thank you."

"Daddy," Sammy said excitedly, "I had a dream I was a dump truck! You were a fire truck and Maven was a Barbie car and Hannah was a race car and we were looking for buried treasure."

"Did we find it?" I asked, taking a sip.

"Uh-huh," he said with a nod. "It was full of *duh-floons!*"

I laughed. "Doubloons?"

"That's what I said! And then the bad pirates came, and you fought them with a sword."

"I thought I was a fire truck. Did I have hands?"

"No, we turned into people again, and you wore a funny hat."

"Did we beat the pirates?"

He grinned. "We stole their ship! It was a good dream. I'll draw you a picture, Daddy. That way, you can see."

"*Arr, matey, that sounds like music to me ears,*" I cawed in my best pirate voice. "Everybody ready for school?"

Sammy pushed his plate away and hopped off his seat. "Yep, look!" He modeled his little button-down, pointing one foot out and, then the other to display his shoes which were neatly tied. "I tied them myself! Hannah showed me! She's smart, Daddy. Really smart."

"So are you, bud." I stood and held my hand out, palm up.

He slapped it as hard as he could, and I shook it out, sucking in a breath through my teeth.

He looked so proud of himself, I could barely stand it.

Hannah picked Maven up from her booster seat and set her down. She was also fully clothed all the way down to her little pink shoes with sparkles on them.

"Mind if I walk with you all today?" I asked.

Sammy cheered, and Hannah froze for a split second, quickly enough that I wasn't sure if I'd imagined it, before turning to button Maven's cardigan.

"That would be nice," she said enigmatically as she shepherded the children out of the kitchen.

I tried to ignore the warm flush of disappointment.

What'd you expect, Charlie old boy? Did you want her to jump up and down and giggle? Get a grip, man.

I downed as much coffee as I could and passed the mug to Katie, who took it with a knowing smile.

"Have a good day, Charlie."

I offered a smile that told her to leave it be. The last thing I needed was Katie making things harder than they were.

"You too, nosy."

"Who? Me?" She tittered innocently.

"Ha. *Bye*, Katie."

She laughed as I walked away.

They were in the foyer, Hannah helping the kids get their coats and backpacks on. I pulled on my suit coat and then my wool coat, reaching for my scarf. When I looked over, I caught Hannah's eyes roaming, and she flushed, turning for her own coat, shielding her face from me.

It shouldn't have made me feel like a goddamn king, but it did.

I slung on my leather bag and picked up Maven, who rested her head in the crook of my neck, thumb in her mouth. And we headed out into the crisp fall morning together.

We didn't speak for a little while. Sammy filled the air with questions and curious chatter for a block or more, and Hannah answered every one with patience and genuine interest.

I found myself wondering just how such a person existed. Even at my best, I had limits to how many questions I could answer in a five-minute span.

Sammy launched into the chorus of "Yellow Submarine," which was quiet enough that I could chance a conversation with Hannah.

"Anything planned for today while the kids are in school?"

She shrugged, her arm swinging with Sammy's as he marched next to her in time to the words. "I have some postcards to write, and I thought I might bake a little something. Katie told me about some specialty shops nearby, a new cheese shop I'd like to visit, too."

"I wondered where you'd gotten quark cheese. I'd never even *heard* of quark."

Hannah chuckled. "Katie picked it up for me. We Dutch love our cheese. I hope they have imported cheese. American cheese is …" Her nose wrinkled.

"Plastic?"

A nod. "It's even shiny, like wax food. Things are just different here."

"Different good?"

She shrugged. "Just different. Faster. Easier in a lot of ways. Things are convenient and accessible. But that also sort of makes you feel like you should be able to get what you want, whenever you want it."

"As opposed to …"

"Well, for instance, in my town, nothing is open on Sundays but restaurants. If you don't have bread, you don't have bread. You make do with what you *do* have."

I laughed at that. "Yeah, Americans wouldn't go for that."

"Exactly. It's convenient, but … I don't know. It's just a different state of mind in Holland, I suppose. Slower-paced, easygoing. No one works more than thirty or *maybe* forty hours a week."

Even the thought of working so little was borderline obscene. "Man, they are doing life right."

"There's no right or wrong, just *different*."

"Yeah, well, their *different* sounds like *voodoo magic* to me."

Sammy's song and marching escalated in volume violence until he was jerking Hannah's arm and slapping his sneakers against the pavement. She joined in singing, slowing him down enough that he wouldn't dislocate her arm.

Another block brought us to their daycare, and Hannah followed me inside. The kids doled out hugs and kisses before running in to join their friends. Well, Sammy ran, and Maven walked in with a furtive glance over her shoulder. We waved, which seemed to fortify her, and she toddled away.

I ushered Hannah into the lobby with my hand on the small of her back; it wasn't intentional, just an instinct, the desire to guide her and touch her overriding any thoughts I might actually have on the matter. But Hannah didn't stiffen or pull away. She looked up at me and smiled.

The girl behind the counter at the front desk did little to hide her judgment as I signed in the kids, pinning me with a look that said she could see straight through me.

And I couldn't find it in me to care.

We said goodbye to the curious counter girl and walked outside, pausing on the sidewalk, facing each other.

"Well, good luck with your cheese," I said stupidly.

She laughed. "Good luck with your contracts."

I chuffed. "Please, contracts are the easy part. It's the twelve-hour negotiations I'm about to walk into that have me squirrelly."

Another moment of silence passed as we watched each other.

I wanted to touch her again. I wanted to talk to her, to hear her laugh, to —

I broke away, my effort toward being responsible. "Don't have too much fun. I'll see you later."

"Tonight?" she asked.

And my heart skittered at the optimism I heard there.

"I wouldn't count on it, but I hope I'm wrong."

She smiled. I smiled.

And I stepped away, not trusting myself to say more. "Have a good day, Hannah."

"You too, Charlie."

My mind was still pointed back at her as I walked away, as if it wanted to watch her go. It was unfair to her and even to me to consider her in any way but the professional one, but I couldn't seem to help myself.

I tried to tell myself that it was just because she was the first woman I'd been attracted to in so long. I wanted to believe it was just that I'd had that door closed for a long time—even when I was still with Mary—and now that the *possibility* had arisen, I'd jumped into the feeling too soon.

I told myself it was a fluke, that it meant nothing, and as I walked away, I thought I'd maybe begun to convince myself that it was true. But that was just another lie in a long line I'd been telling myself.

HANNAH

I walked away from Charlie, heart thumping too hard.

How he did that to me, I'd never understand.

In two weeks, Charlie had changed, the shift so slight but strong and swift. It had started with the night we baked *kwarktaarts*, the first time that he joined in on the fun, relaxing, slowing down, even if only for a moment. On the weekends after that night, he would always stop for lunch and dinner and would handle the kids through baths and bedtime. I'd shadow him at his request, but he didn't really need my help. Charlie knew what to do. He only needed to believe that he knew what to do.

A small part of me whispered that he'd only asked for my help as a way to keep me close by. But the truth was that Charlie was afraid and unsure. And because I saw his uncertainty, there was only one thing to do; I had to help. So, I'd step in when he deferred to me and offer encouragement where I could. I believed in him, and it seemed he was beginning to believe in himself.

He was happy, I realized, giving me a little glimpse into another version of him that seemed to have disappeared over time. But as it resurfaced, it was changing him, even on the outside. I only wondered how it was changing him beyond what I could see.

And through it all, we'd become friends. The bruises on my heart left by Quinton had faded until they were almost gone, the pain all but forgotten.

Charlie had completely disarmed me. And with that openness came a different sort of danger.

Sometimes, things would happen when nothing happened at all. Something hidden in a stolen glance, a change in our breaths, in the brushing of hands when we passed a child from one to the other. I knew I should try to keep my distance, keep as much space between us as I could, but instead, we would circle each other in a dance I found myself not wanting to end.

It's harmless, I told myself.

Neither of us would act on it; I was convinced. I wouldn't do anything to endanger my position. This was the first time since I'd come to America that I felt good, safe, happy, and I didn't want to lose that.

And so I pushed thoughts of him away, though they never stayed gone long. But I'd keep trying.

Nothing good could come from traveling that path.

A little while later, I found myself in the small cheese shop—which was as glorious as Katie had promised—with a full basket and a happy heart. I didn't look up when the bell over the door rang, not until I heard *his* voice.

"Hannah?"

My grip on the basket tightened, the muscles in my body flexing on reflex, and I looked up to find Quinton standing at my side.

He was so tall, his hair dark as pitch and eyes the color of ice—so pale, they were closer to gray than blue. His jaw—a hard, dominate line—was set, his lips curled into a smile that sent a trickling coldness through me with every racing heartbeat.

I couldn't speak.

"It's good to see you," he said genially. "I didn't realize you had come back from Holland."

I opened my mouth, dry as bone, summoning the words through my shock. "Yes, only just," I lied. "I was told my old position had been filled."

"It has. And you've found another job, I suppose?"

I nodded. "How are the children?" I asked, desperate to fill the air with enough pleasantries to be able to get away.

"Fine. Listen, I'm sorry about what happened and all."

Nothing about him spoke of the truth—not his eyes locked on mine, not the edge in his voice, not the set of his shoulders.

But I said, "Thank you," all the same. Accepting his apology was beyond me.

"I'm glad you're back. Weird, running into you," he said on a chuckle, slipping his hand into the pocket of his slacks. "I thought I saw you from across the street and had to see if it was really you. Imagine that."

I smiled, lips together and tight. "Yes, what a coincidence." I took a step back. "Well, I have to—"

"Of course. I should go too. It's good to see you, Hannah," he said, his eyes holding me for a moment before he nodded once and turned to walk away, leaving me standing stunned in the shop.

It wasn't until the door closed and he was out of sight that I moved, heading to the counter to pay with shaking hands and a spinning mind.

Something told me it was no coincidence at all that I'd seen him.

I didn't feel safe again until I was home with the door closed and locked behind me. Panic had driven me to walk back too fast, my eyes scanning the sidewalk in front of me and across the street, looking for him so intently that I imagined a few people were him who weren't.

So I spent the day inside with Katie, baking and talking and busying my hands and distracting my mind. And with every hour, I convinced myself I'd overreacted.

What could he have possibly wanted from me? Surely he'd had no expectations, no offer to make that I could entertain, and he had to understand that. Surely he wouldn't have sought me out to hurt me. It had to have been chance, nothing more.

If I hadn't promised Lysanne I'd meet her at the park, I would have picked up the children and gone straight back home. But instead, I packed up a snack and picked up the kids early to meet her.

Hand in hand, the kids and I headed to the park where we found Lysanne waiting at the sandbox where her youngest ward, Charlotte, sat playing with plastic buckets and shovels in primary colors. Sammy took off running for the slide where Lysanne's older ward, Sydney, waved at him, and Maven headed for the sandbox with me.

Lysanne and I greeted each other with kisses on the cheeks as Maven sat down next to Charlotte and began to dig.

"I brought you something," I said with a smile.

Lysanne lit up as we sat. "Oh, I love presents."

I opened up the bag and retrieved a container, popping off the lid to reveal a cheese and sausage spread.

Her mouth opened, her eyes big. "Is that Leyden cheese?" she breathed.

I nodded, beaming. "Mmhmm!"

"Oh my God," she said as she reached in to pick up a piece of speckled cheese. She popped it in her mouth, and her eyes closed in ecstasy. "Hannah, oh my God."

"I know!" I practically giggled the words.

"Where in the world did you find this?" She went in for another piece, this time stacking it on a slice of sausage.

"A cheese shop." I took a bite of my own.

"It's incredible," she said with her mouth full, loading another stack in before she swallowed the first.

I laughed. "I have bread too, and crackers."

"Ugh, I could kiss you."

"Maybe swallow first."

Lysanne laughed, and I unpacked the rest of the food. The girls approached, and we offered cheddar and crackers.

I watched Lysanne for a moment before taking a breath. "Something happened today," I started, not knowing how to even bring it up.

She didn't inquire, only raised one dark brow.

"I ran into Quinton."

Her jaw, opened in anticipation of cheese, dropped a centimeter more. "No."

"Yes."

"What did he want?"

"He said he saw me and wanted to say hello. He asked about Holland and my job, though only a little. I tried to get out of the conversation as quickly as I could."

"Do you think he was telling the truth? Surely he wasn't following you, right?"

"I …" I shook my head, not wanting to even consider it. "I don't know. Whatever could he be doing in a cheese shop on a Tuesday morning?"

Her hand dropped to her lap. "What are you going to do?"

"What can I do? He didn't do anything wrong, didn't say anything that wasn't all right."

"Well, he assaulted you, so it isn't like he's completely innocent," she volleyed.

"No, I know, but …" I sighed a deep, long breath. "There's not much to be done. He greeted me in a public place and with no intentions, none that I could see."

"I don't like it."

"I don't either."

"Well, hopefully that's the end of it," she said.

And we both smiled, the gestures thin and transparent.

"So, how is *Charlie*?" she sang, batting her lashes like a cartoon.

"He's *fine*," I answered pointedly, though I had to chuckle.

"You like him."

"I barely know him. And even if I did think anything more of him, I wouldn't do anything about it. That's not why I'm here."

She snickered. "No, you're here to, what? Find Dutch cheese and take care of someone else's children and absolutely not because you're hiding from your family?"

My cheeks warmed up. "I'm not hiding from them."

"You're hiding from the bakery."

"That was all decided a long time ago," I dodged.

"I'm only saying, I understand it's hard, knowing you can't run the shop like you want, but I they'd let you work there at least."

I shook my head. "I know, but … Lysanne, there's no room for me there, and that's all right."

She gave me a look.

"It is," I said as I covered her hand with mine. "For now, where I am is just fine. And it was *your* idea for me to come here, so you should be careful throwing around ideas on me leaving."

"Yes, it was my idea. I missed you. I'm selfish that way."

I laughed, shaking my head.

A girl walked around the corner, pushing a stroller. She had a haughty look about her as she scanned the park, landing on Lysanne. She tried to smile, but the expression was puckered and sour.

"Oh God. It's Claudette. Wave."

We both waved, passing fake smiles back to her. She kept going, moving to the other end of the park.

"Who's that?" I asked.

Lysanne rolled her eyes. "French trollop. She was an au pair—before she slept with the father for a *whole year*. He'd sneak into her room almost every night. Can you believe that?"

I blinked at her. "That's horrible."

She waved a dismissive hand. "The mother was sleeping with the gardener, so they were at scratch. They divorced, and now, Claudette is married to him and had his baby. *There's* one woman who will never, ever have an au pair."

A laugh burst out of me. "I can't believe that."

"Believe it," Lysanne said and reached in for more cheese. "Mmm, gouda."

"Is it really that common for au pairs to sleep with their employers?"

"Uh, yes. Think about it," she said, gesticulating as she explained. "You've got this girl; she's young and exotic, from another country, and she lives in your house. Things aren't what they used to be with your wife, stress of children and jobs and all that. It's a recipe for disaster. A German au pair I used to know said her bosses asked her to have a threesome. Can you imagine?"

"No, I can't."

"Being a parent is a hard, lonely business, even when you're married. Everyone feels like they're doing it alone, even when they're working together. Throw a younger girl, a girl who's *free*—that's part of the allure too, I think—and it's hard not to fantasize, I'm sure. Makes me glad my boss is ugly."

"You're awful," I said, though I laughed around the words.

"I don't think I'd ever hire an au pair. A nanny, maybe, since at least they don't usually live with you, but not an au pair." Lysanne finally slowed down on the cheese but picked up a piece of bread and nibbled on the corner. "How long do you think you can hold out with Charlie?"

Another flush bloomed on my cheeks, warm and tingling. "Really, Lysanne."

"I'm serious! There's no real reason you can't."

"Of course there is. He's going through a divorce. He works all the time. He's my boss. He's older—"

"I think they prefer *experienced*."

I rolled my eyes.

"And don't think I didn't notice that you didn't mention that you don't like him."

"It's nothing. It means nothing other than I think he's attractive. I like him. I'll even admit that I admire him, and he's become my friend. But it ends there. There's nothing more to it than that and there never will be, so please leave it alone."

She held up her hands, palms out, in surrender. "All right. I would say, *The lady doth protest too much*, but I'm afraid you'll take the cheese away, and this is the best thing to happen to me all week."

And I gladly took the exit from the conversation, turning us to other subjects while doing my best to ignore how right she was.

Dancing Animals
CHARLIE

The rest of the week passed by at breakneck speed, powered by my team nearing the end of an acquisition that demanded an outrageous number of hours. Twice I'd slept in the office—though maybe *sleep* was a generous term for the four-hour nap I'd snuck in. I'd barely seen the kids, which I hated, nor had I seen much of Hannah, which I also hated.

Time and space hadn't banished her from my thoughts.

It was always in the quiet hours when my tired brain found itself idle that she snuck into my mind. While at work, I'd wonder what she was doing, wonder how the kids were. Throughout the days, our conversations had been limited to texts; she'd sent me photos of crafts, the kids baking, videos of them saying goodnight, and Halloween trick-or-treating photos—my plans to join them annihilated by an emergency meeting that lasted until after midnight.

Hannah was never in the pictures other than the occasional hand or her voice laughing or prompting them to speak. And every little glimpse I got of her would reignite that desperate wonder I couldn't seem to shake.

I came home late that night, creeping up the creaky stairs as quietly as I could. I'd been so aware of her presence—her coat hanging next to mine, her shoes under the bench, the flowers in the kitchen, which were daisies now—as if every part of me turned its focus to the woman down the stairs. But I didn't stop walking, didn't stop moving until I was safely between my sheets.

As tired as I was, I couldn't fall asleep, her face in my thoughts, thinking of the things I'd say to her in the morning, imagining the conversations we'd have, the moments we'd have.

I'd found myself living for those moments.

That was the worst part—the anticipation of seeing her, the admission that I looked forward to it, *needed* it.

At that, I cursed myself and pushed thoughts of her away, though they only bobbed back up again to mock me.

She's too young, I told myself.
You pay her to work for you.
You're just lonely, Charlie boy.
She's just different, that's all. New.
It's a fantasy, Charlie. Just pretend, only make-believe. Put it away.
She wouldn't want you and your baggage anyway.

And that was the loop of self-flagellation I fell asleep to.

When I woke that Sunday morning on the heels of a solid eight hours of sleep and with such a brutal week behind me, it was with a smile on my face and a spring in my step. I felt *rejuvenated,* if not still physically tired, and Hannah and the kids would be home with me all day. I had to work—I needed to, as the contracts on my desk were due for approval first thing in the morning—but I'd see them all. My mind spun with imaginings of *moments.*

Dangerous and stupid.

But logic didn't apply. For the first time in a very long time, I was reminded that I could feel, that I could want, that I was a man, not a robot. Not just a father or a cuckold or a workaholic. It was a reminder that I was alive.

I'd unknowingly allowed myself the luxury of daydreaming, stoking the tiny flame of desire for her. I only hoped I could keep that fire contained and in check, well within the ruts I'd dug to keep it penned in. If the wind picked up, if it jumped that boundary, I would be in trouble.

Big trouble.

In any case, I felt like a million bucks when I woke. I whistled as I made my bed and dressed for the day and took the stairs with a little bounce, the sound of Hannah and the kids floating up the stairs to me.

And there was Hannah with my children in the entryway, smiling up at me.

Make that a million and one bucks.

"Daddy!" Sammy called, whipping away from Hannah to run for me just before she could get his jacket on.

He bounded into my arms, and I picked him up.

"Morning, buddy. Where are you guys off to so early?"

"The zoo! Can you come with us?"

I couldn't. I had a metric ton of paperwork to get through, and there was absolutely no way I could take a day off. I couldn't even take a couple of *hours* off.

So I looked at my children and Hannah, whose faces were hopeful, and gave the only answer I could. "Absolutely. Give me ten minutes."

All three of them lit up like a row of Edison bulbs.

I kissed Sam's temple and set him down, trotting back up the stairs. I ducked into the bathroom to brush my teeth, assessing my scruff and my messy hair. But they seemed all right, and a day awaited. A day off. A day with my kids.

A day with Hannah, a little voice in my head said.

Shut up, I said back.

When I came downstairs, they waited patiently on the bench under the hooks where coats and bags hung—Maven in Hannah's lap, Sammy talking about giraffes.

"Hannah, how do you say giraffe?"

"Easy. *Giraffe.*"

"*Gee-raf-fuh*" he echoed, pronouncing it just like her but without the soft roll on the R.

"Well done."

"Did you know a giraffe's tongue is one-and-one-half-foots long?"

"Really?" Hannah said, seemingly enthralled.

"Uh-huh. And they only sleep two hours every day."

"It's like a nap."

He nodded. "I wish I could just sleep that long, and the rest of the time I could play, play, play." With every *play,* he jumped.

Hannah and I laughed, and the three of them stood as I pulled on my coat and took Maven. Hannah grabbed the bag, Sammy took her hand, and I carried the stroller as we headed out. She and I worked around each other, situating the kids, setting Maven up—I buckled her in, and Hannah placed Maven's sippy cup in my waiting hand, hung the bag on the handles, and took the wheel. And with Sammy's hand in mine, we walked toward the subway entrance. We hadn't spoken a word.

I smiled to myself at the easiness of it all, smiled at the crisp fall sky, at the sight of Hannah pushing the stroller and Sammy talking—now about sea otters. Did you know that a group of sea otters in the water was called a raft? Yeah, me neither. My son, the wonder boy.

The train was uncrowded so early on a weekend, and before

long, we were walking up 5th Avenue and into the park. There was a small line—the zoo was just opening—but before the ticket booths unfurled their metal shields, the Delacorte Clock struck ten, and the animals danced.

Maven sat on my shoulders, clapping, and Sammy jumped up and down, giggling, as the clock chimed its song, the bronze sculptures spinning around—bear and kangaroo, penguin and hippo, each playing an instrument. And Hannah's face was just as filled with wonder, turned up to the sight, smile on her lips.

I found myself thirsty for that smile, the sweet simplicity of her joy.

When the song ended, we bought our tickets and moseyed in.

The zoo was small but quaint, and I was nearly as enthralled as the kids. They'd been before with Elliot, but I hadn't been since years before. Of course, now that I was older, things were different, and my perspective along with it. It was the way of the world, I supposed, the joy of seeing something through the eyes of your children, experiencing the newness and possibilities in life.

And so we made our way around, starting with the sea lions in the center of the park, through the bats and lemurs and snakes. Did you know snakes didn't have eyelids? I could have guessed, but it was unnerving to learn it from my five-year-old all the same. Past the monkeys and snow leopards we went, Sammy asking for the animal names in Dutch all the while, which were strikingly similar to their English versions. Except snake, which was apparently called a *slang* in Dutch and was pronounced way too close to *schlong* for me to be happy about my three-year-old daughter repeating it on a loop, which she did—and with enthusiasm.

When we reached the grizzly bear, both kids shot up to the rail, watching the beast lumber around his habitat, batting at a large red ball.

I hung back, eyes on the kids, my heart soft and quiet and full. So much of this I'd missed, so many afternoons at the park and making pasta necklaces and finger painting. As much as I'd been trying to make it up to them, it didn't feel like enough.

They were growing up, and I had been missing everything. It seemed like only a moment ago that I had rocked Maven with a bottle in her mouth, her little fingers gripping one of mine as her big, dark eyes watched me, while I listened to the soft suckling noises, the rhythm broken only by her sighing breath. A deep longing spread through my chest, its roots twisting around my stomach.

"I'm a terrible father," I said quietly, wishing for forgiveness with the confession, though I knew there would be none.

Hannah turned her face to mine but said nothing.

I kept my eyes on the kids, not wanting to admit it aloud but compelled to all the same. "It took my wife leaving for me to realize that I wanted to be more present in their lives. Five years of neglect, five years of stumbling through fatherhood and hiding behind work. How horrible is that?"

She only watched me. I could see her eyes out of the corner of mine, and they were sad.

"I was always too busy. It was always *later*. Tomorrow. Next weekend. Never now. Never yes. Only no." I took a breath and let it out. "The problem is, I can't have what I want. Even considering it now seems silly, like a daydream. I *can't* be there, not like I want to be. I shouldn't have even come today." I sounded pitiful and wretched, which was exactly how I felt. "They deserve more."

She reached for my forearm and clasped it, an act not intended to be anything but comforting, though I found myself wishing she'd slide her fingers into mine, wondering if it would ease my mind and heart.

"You're doing the best you can."

I shook my head. "That's just an excuse, Hannah. I've been using that line for years."

"What I mean is, you are *enough*," she said without doubt.

I chanced a look at her, and her eyes held me still.

"For more than a month now, I've watched you with your children. I've watched you play with them and listen to them and hold them and take care of them. I've seen you in the moments you don't think anyone's watching, the moments when you're happy and sad all at once, the moments when it's clear just how much you love them. *Anyone* who saw you with them would agree that they are the most important part of your life. And a terrible father wouldn't worry if he was a terrible father."

"But it's never enough. I've changed. I want more. They need more. And I can't truly give it to them."

"Charlie, this is your lot, and you're surviving it as best you can."

It was the truth and it wasn't. I should have made more time and long before now. I should have. But I hadn't.

I swallowed hard, but the lump lodged itself back in my throat.

"I wish that were true. I wish there were a way to … to …" I shook my head. "It's stupid. I'm not one to wish for things I can't have."

She nodded, her eyes sad, full of acceptance and recognition. "I understand how you feel. And I'm sorry."

It was so quiet, so simple, two little words that said a dozen different things but solved nothing other than a brief moment of companionship, the feeling of being heard and understood. And that would have to be enough.

I thanked her with a smile, resisting the urge to hug her, to pull her into me. Instead, I turned back to my children and scooped them up, one on each hip and the promise of cotton candy on my lips, and Hannah followed us with the empty stroller, smiling again.

Always smiling.

Just Two People
HANNAH

The day had been absolutely lovely.

Cotton candy in hand, we'd walked out the gates, pausing to watch the clock chime once again, the parade of animals circling to a different song than the one before. Charlie had noted with the same matter-of-factness of his son that the clock had over forty different songs, chiming at half-hour intervals all day.

Next had been the carousel. Sammy had chosen a midnight steed, and I had taken the one next to him.

Charlie had stood between Sammy and Maven, a protective hand on her back, his face alight as he smiled and laughed, reminding them to feed carrots to their horses after they said, "Hi-yah," and, "Giddyup," to pet their manes and flick their reins as we went up and down, round and round, the world whizzing past us in a blur.

We'd walked home through the park, stopping at the Bethesda Terrace where we ate hot dogs and the kids marveled at the fountain.

Sammy had walked the edge, and Maven had leaned over, squealing as she dipped her fingers in the cold water.

All the while, I'd considered Charlie, considered the changes I'd seen in him. For a moment, he'd made time for the children, and in that, he'd found happiness. But it had slipped away from him again the second his job demanded his full and undivided attention a few weeks before. He'd been slowly reclaiming his time ever since.

The job that was the source of his pain, the thing that made him feel like less than he was, that dashed his dreams and stole his time.

And I hated the sadness that had found its way back into his eyes even if only for a moment.

By the time we made it home, it was after five. The kids were tired and cold, so I set them up in the living room with the television and a fire, making my way into the kitchen when they were settled.

Charlie had already pulled out containers of uncooked food that Katie had left with a notecard taped to the top with instructions.

I moved to his side to help.

"Ah, ah, ah," he warned, twisting to keep the containers in his hand out of my reach. "Sit." He nodded to the island where a glass of wine waited in front of a stool.

"Charlie, let me help," I said on a laugh, trying to reach around him.

He only shook his head and held the containers away with his long arms. "If I can't cook this completely prepped and simplified meal that Katie left me—which includes instructions a small child could follow—I have more to worry about than I thought. Please, sit."

I shook my head with a chuckle, but I did as he'd asked and took my seat, much to his satisfaction.

The smile on his face made him look younger, almost boyish as he began popping the lids off the containers.

I picked up the wine and took a sip, the crispness of it sweet. I felt myself relax, leaning on the island, watching Charlie as he poured oil into the warm pan and then the vegetables with a sizzle.

"So, you've never told me why you and your friend decided to come to America to au pair."

"Well, we've been friends since primary school. She decided not to go to university; she wanted to travel. So, she nannied for a bit to save money before signing on with an agency. And off she went. The begging for me to follow came within hours."

"She wore you down, huh?" he asked, pushing the vegetables around in the pan with a wooden spoon before putting a lid on it.

I smiled. "I'm not terribly difficult to convince, and she's very persuasive. I was still finishing school, but once it was over … well, I thought traveling would be just the thing."

"The idea of being finished with school so early is almost unimaginable. Law school aged me ten years." He turned and leaned against the counter, picking up his glass of wine. "What's your degree in?"

"Education. I'm to be a teacher."

He smiled, and warmth spread through my chest. I took a sip of wine to cool it down.

"I can't imagine a more perfect job for you."

I kept my eyes trained on my glass, as if setting it down required all my thoughtful attention. "Yes, I suppose."

His smile faded. "You don't want to teach?"

"It's not that. It's just …" I didn't want to answer or admit the reason aloud.

"The bakery?"

It was my turn to smile, but it was small and pained. "It was never meant to be my dream. I could work there, I'm sure, and I would enjoy it well enough. But my parents expected me to go to university, so I did. I finished, like I was supposed to. But when it came time to look for a job, I felt … I wanted …" I drew in a breath and let it out. "I wanted to run away. I wasn't ready to decide. My parents liken it to a holiday, I think. A little bit of wandering before I settle in."

He nodded, his eyes heavy with understanding. "Expectations aren't easy. The pressure, the obligation, is almost enough to strip you of desire."

I took another sip of my wine to busy myself.

"So, what *do* you want to do?"

"I don't quite know. I keep hoping I'll wake one day and find the answer. Part of me wonders if I'm not happier in the dark. Being here is a respite, and when I go home, I'll feel like I have to do as I'm told."

"Do you always do what you're told?"

I met his eyes. "Yes. But only because it's not unreasonable. I do as I'm told because I don't mind. I knew I needed a degree, that my life would be easier if I had one. I knew I would like teaching children because I love them, and I'm good at it. When my brothers and sister were little, I took care of them because I had to, yes, but also because I wanted to, because it fulfilled me and made me happy. Being helpful makes me happy. Do you understand?"

"I do," he said simply. And the weight in his answer was enough to explain how he felt completely. "Did you always enjoy working with kids?"

"I did. Caring for my little brothers was like a dream come true for my teenage self. Diapers and prams and going on walks and playing at the park."

"Were the kids at your last job a nightmare? Is that why you left?"

I stilled, even my heart, just for a beat. "There were a lot of reasons it didn't work out," I lied. There had only been one.

His brow rose with one corner of his lips. "Let me guess; they were gluten-free?"

"Something like that." I laughed, anxious to change the subject. Because the last thing I wanted to discuss at the end of such a lovely day was Quinton. "How about you? Why did you choose law?"

He took a sip of his wine and set it down before turning back to add the chicken to the pan. "The real answer? Money. I wanted to be *successful*, and in my peabrained, youthful mind, that meant money. I had no idea what success really meant or happiness either. Lesson learned." He pushed the mix around for a few seconds, seemingly lost in thought. "I enjoyed school though. I love problem-solving, finding answers, fixing things. And I do a lot of that now, but it leaves me no time for anything else. I want more out of life, but I'm trapped where I am."

"I know how you feel."

He smiled at me over his shoulder. "Yeah, I think you do." The lid was placed on the pan again, and he turned back to me. "I know this is a terribly American thing to say, but you speak English really well. I don't know any other languages other than some Spanish. The useful stuff, like swear words and how to ask for more beer. I also have a couple of gems in my repertoire like, *No me gusta la lucha libre,* and *Donde está la biblioteca?*"

I laughed fully at that, a little louder than manners defined. "Well, I don't like wrestling either, and I always think one should know where the nearest library is."

"It's important information. I knew you'd get it."

My cheeks were warm and still smiling. "Lysanne and I used to read romance novels in English when we were teenagers. Everyone takes English in school, starting around when we're ten or eleven, and almost everyone speaks very good English. So many Americans and Brits move there, too. In Amsterdam, *everyone* speaks it. Where I'm from, just south of Amsterdam, most people do. Not as well— we don't have as much practice—but Lysanne was obsessed with America when we were younger, so I think I might know more slang and turns of phrase than most. It's no wonder she ended up moving here. I wasn't surprised in the least."

"So you learned English from reading romance novels and, what? Watching MTV?"

I nodded. "And we'd speak it to each other all the time. So, thanks to her, I've had a bit of practice."

"Do you speak it to her now that you're here?"

"No," I said, chuckling. "We always speak Dutch now. I think she misses home a little. I thought she might fall to pieces when I brought her *leidsekaas*."

"Which one is that?" he asked as he stirred the food again and moved the pan off the burner.

"The one that's a little spicy."

"I almost fell to pieces over that one too."

He moved to the cabinet for plates, and I slid off my stool to help, taking the plates.

"So, *kaas* is cheese, right?"

"Ja."

He smiled and followed me with forks and napkins. "What's chicken?"

"Kip. Dat is een kipfilet." I pointed at the pan.

"That is a chicken fillet?" he guessed.

"Ja. Goed gedaan, Charlie!" I praised. *"Wat is dat?"* I pointed at a plate.

"I have no idea."

"Dat is een borden."

He took the new knowledge and held up a fork, his eyes bright. *"Wat is dat?"*

"Wat is dis?" I corrected. *"Dat is een vork."*

"Vork," he said with a smile and laid out cutlery behind me as we walked around the table. "It sounds like English."

"It's very similar, yes. It's the closest language to English in the world. The grammar is almost as complicated, too," I joked and set the last plate on the table.

Charlie caught up with me, still smiling, still looking at me with endless eyes. "Now I know why Sammy's always asking you to translate for him."

He made to move past me—we were between the table and the window—reaching for my arms as he brushed behind me, his body against mine in only the smallest of ways, but I felt every place where he touched me long after he walked away.

"I'll get the kids," I said a little breathlessly and hurried out of the kitchen before he could turn or answer.

And just like that, nothing was simple, the lines I'd thought were between us erased with a day spent together. Because the truth was that it no longer felt like he was my boss. It didn't only feel like he was my friend; it felt like more—much more. And that notion gave me pause, forced me back a step.

I loved my job. I loved the children, and I cared for Charlie. And, for the first time since coming to America, I didn't want to leave.

If I crossed that line, I might have to after all.

As we ate, I watched him, listened to him, laughed with him. I couldn't deny that we'd turned a dangerous corner. When he smiled at something I'd said, the corners of his dark eyes would crinkle, and I'd find myself beaming at him.

Charlie was beautiful. He was smart and giving and charming.

And he was beyond my reach.

But sitting there across from each other, we were just two people in a kitchen, drinking wine and laughing. Everything about him said *yes*, and I found myself leaning into the word, wishing I could say it, wishing he would.

There were so many reasons we couldn't, reasons I used to bolster my crumbling resolve, stacking them up like sandbags full of holes.

We were nearly finished eating when Maven's exhaustion from

the day and missed nap won over. She slapped her little hands on the table, but her fingers caught the lip of her plate, flipping it into the air with a spray of peas like little missiles.

I moved quickly, setting my napkin on my plate as I stood and reached for her. She wailed, her face pink and mouth in a little circle, sparkling tears rolling down her cheeks as I soothed her. It was too loud for me to hear Charlie approaching, but he was at my side, reaching for her, and she reached for him, curling into him as she popped her thumb into her mouth and cried around it.

"Come on, baby," he said gently, rubbing her back with his big hand. "You all finished, Sammy?"

"Yep!" he said with a pop of the *P*, jumping out of his chair.

"Let me go bathe them," I offered.

But he shook his head. "I've got it. Thanks, Hannah."

I felt a strange mixture of pride and rejection. "Of course," I said, my face flushing.

He saw it and turned to me, his eyes soft. "Pour me another glass, would you? I'll be just a minute."

And I smiled back, hating myself for feeling relieved. "All right."

Charlie walked away with his children, and I tried to clear my head by cleaning up dinner, my mind and heart colliding in my noisy thoughts.

You don't belong here, I reminded myself as I cleaned up Maven's mess.

Find a way to put the wall back up, I thought as I stacked the plates and carried them to the sink.

You can't have him, I tried to convince my heart as I washed and rinsed and put everything away.

I shouldn't have had any wine, my thin resolve too easily swayed with its aid. I should have gone to my room. I should have been smart and told myself with some amount of command to stop what I was doing and find a way out.

But instead, I poured another glass for Charlie and one for myself. *Because he asked me*, I told myself. Because he needed a friend. Because everything would work out. He would never broach the boundary even if I wanted him to.

My feet ached from the day, and the kitchen seemed too hard, too stiff. So I walked into the living room and sat, not bothering with the light. The fire was enough. I watched it crackle and burn, thinking. I was thinking so hard in fact that, once again, I didn't hear Charlie approach, didn't register him until he walked around the couch, looking tired himself.

He took the seat next to me and picked up his wine, saying nothing for a moment, both of us lost in the orange and red coals of the logs and flickering flames.

Put up the wall.

I smiled politely and shifted to sit a little straighter. "The kids went to bed all right?"

He nodded, his face content and soft. "They did. I like putting them to bed. Is that weird?"

I chuckled. "Not at all."

His lips tilted into a smile.

"I straightened up the kitchen. Thank you for dinner."

"Thank you for your company and for spending the day with us."

"I was glad to. It's my job after all."

He turned to meet my eyes, searching them for an answer to a question I hadn't heard him ask, not out loud. *Is it?* they seemed to say.

But it was, and we both knew it.

I took a breath, fixing the smile in place. "I should go."

"Where? To your room, alone? To bed? It's not even seven." His voice was light, but his face wasn't. His face begged me to stay.

When I didn't respond quickly enough, he filled the opening with a gentle command. "Finish your wine. Sit with me."

And my paper-thin composure rumpled uselessly. "All right."

I settled back into the couch and turned my eyes to the fire once more.

Charlie didn't say anything for a minute or two, the two of us sipping our wine and sitting close enough that I could reach out and touch him. But I didn't dare.

"I can't remember the last time I spent a whole day with the kids," he said. "That World's Best Dad mug is just for show."

He was trying to joke, but the words were heavy with regret.

"It felt good, *right*, but it hurt, too. It reminded me of everything I'd been missing."

"But you're here now, Charlie. You're here now."

"If it's not too late."

"It's never too late to change your mind."

He considered that for a moment. "Sammy's five, and Mary and I never took him anywhere together," he started, pausing. "Well, that's not exactly true. Once, when he was a baby, we went to the aquarium. He was too little, I realize that now, and he cried the entire time we were there. Mary was miserable. By the time we got home, we were both fried. We got in a huge fight the second we walked in the door. I think we both felt like failures, to be honest. But, in the end, we never even tried again." He turned to me. "We never tried. Maybe that was our trouble all along."

His face was sad and beautiful, half cast in shadow, and I held my glass with two hands to stop myself from reaching for him.

"I don't know what I'm supposed to be. Am I supposed to be sad that she left? Because I am—but because of the kids, not for myself. They haven't seen their mother in nine months. She won't speak to me, doesn't seem to care about them, and I feel like I pass them off to whoever will take them. And I've put my own wants and wishes in a box and thrown it in the river."

"Do you miss her?" I asked.

"Not at all. That's the worst part. I was angry. God, was I angry. She ..." He paused, swallowing. "Did Katie tell you?"

"A little," I admitted.

He turned his attention back to the fire. "She was sleeping with my best friend. I should have known. Should have fucking known," he said quietly. "Maybe I just didn't want to see. Maybe I knew all along."

I didn't speak, just waited, my eyes tracing the line of his profile, over his worried brow and long nose, over the slope of his lips and strong chin, shining with blond stubble.

"When she left, I thought it would set me free. I was glad to have her presence gone from the house, not realizing just how hard it had been to be near her, not understanding how she'd affected me without my knowing. I'd been sinking, drowning. And she didn't care—didn't care about me, didn't care about our children. She only cared about herself, even now. She's never even signed the divorce papers; that's how little she can be bothered."

An unwelcome pain settled into my chest.

"She didn't show up to the custody hearing, just let me have them. And I'm glad, as guilty as that makes me feel. It's almost easier with her gone completely. I don't know what kind of hell I'd have gone through if she'd fought me the whole way."

"What happens when someone doesn't sign divorce papers?" I asked quietly, curiously.

"She had a deadline to send them in, and when it passed, there was a waiting period before I can file for a default ruling. Basically, it means she's waived her rights, and those rights have defaulted to me. But there's still time. If she shows up, if she decides to fight, she can petition to have the default ruling reversed, and then we'll fight for every scrap. Until it's over, I won't be able to breathe or move on."

"Do you think she will? Do you think she'll fight?"

"Fighting is all I've ever known from her. The fact that she's been silent is the most unnerving part of it all, and it leaves me without any context for what she'll do or what she won't. I sometimes wonder if she's doing this on purpose, if she knows how she's torturing me. She doesn't want me, but she doesn't want to let me go. How fucked up is that?"

He didn't want a response, and I didn't have one to offer.

"To find out that your life is a lie, your marriage a sham … the rug was pulled, and it sent me tumbling down the stairs in slow motion. I didn't know how to deal with it. So, I worked. I worked and worked and left the kids with the nanny and pretended like everything was okay. Some days I feel like it is. But sometimes, I feel like what I've done, who I've become, is irredeemable."

My hand moved to his without my permission, and by the time I realized what I'd done, it was too late to take it back.

He turned to look into my eyes. "Hannah, I …" The words seem to jam in his throat, and he turned his hand under mine to lace our fingers.

"It's all right, Charlie," I said just above a whisper.

"Is it?" he whispered back.

And my heart thumped painfully.

And he was leaning, and I was leaning, and my pulse was racing.

"Yes." It was permission and a plea, a single word heavy with longing and wishes I shouldn't have and shouldn't feel. But I did.

And he answered me with a breath that pulled me into him, millimeter by agonizing millimeter.

I closed my eyes.

I leaned in.

He disappeared, and the loss was instant and sharp.

When I opened my eyes, his were tragically sad and utterly dejected.

"God, Hannah. I'm sorry. I'm so sorry. I can't believe I … I shouldn't have …"

I opened my mouth to speak, but he was already standing, already walking away, already slipping through my fingers.

"It won't happen again," he said with certainty before hurrying away.

And I touched my lips that had almost tasted him and wished he'd whispered a lie.

No Amount of Banketstaaf

HANNAH

I woke the next morning feeling unrested, sleep full of restless dreams I couldn't remember. When I opened my heavy lids and looked up at the molding, my first thought was of Charlie, followed by a hot rush of shame.

I'd come back to my room last night swallowing tears and rejection, bewildered and wounded and confused. I shouldn't have touched him, shouldn't have had so much to drink, shouldn't have gotten so close to his heart. Because the more I knew, the more he told me, every minute we spent together—it only pulled me closer to that line.

I didn't want to want him, but the truth was that I was well past the point of control.

Because I'd wanted him to kiss me. I wanted it still. I'd said yes, and he'd said no. And that was all the answer I needed.

That answer didn't make the truth any easier to bear.

And now, everything would change. We wouldn't spend any more days together without the *no* hanging between us. I wondered if the damage was deeper, if he was upset with me. I wondered if I should leave, wondered if he would fire me.

A desperate, *No,* rushed through me, and I did my best to push the wave of panic down.

There were things I could control and things I couldn't. I would see him when I left my room, and as I lay in a bed that wasn't mine, hair fanned out around me, face turned up to the blank ceiling, I considered what I would say, what he might say.

Stupid, silly girl.

There was really only one answer, one solution. I would hold my head up and focus on my job, which was what I should have been doing all along. I would put up the wall of propriety and expectation and stay firmly on my side of it. And I would hope against all reason that we could move on and pretend like last night had never happened.

This was the thought that bolstered me as I climbed out of bed and dressed for the day. It was the sentiment that kept my nerves tamped down as I climbed the stairs, bracing myself to see Charlie like I was waiting for the guillotine to drop.

But he wasn't on the main floor. Katie waved at me from the kitchen as she moved biscuits onto a tray but offered nothing in the way of information. I climbed the stairs to wake the children, glancing at Charlie's room. The door hung open, his bed empty and rumpled.

He was already gone. Over everything else, I felt relief by a large margin, though a sliver of disappointment made its presence known just as well, perhaps to spite my good intentions.

I turned the whole of my attention to the children, busying myself with collecting them, dressing them, and ushering them downstairs for breakfast.

Katie and I moved about each other, situating the children, and when they were happily eating, she offered a seat at the island where a cup of tea waited for me.

"Thank you," I said as I sat, wrapping my hands around the warm mug.

"You're welcome. Charlie left just as I was coming in. Strange to not have him here in the mornings like he has been."

I didn't know what it was about the way she'd said it, but the statement felt loaded with questions, her eyes full of some knowing, and it made me wonder what Charlie had said to her on his way out.

I tried to smile. "He must have a lot of work to tend to today."

"Yes, he must," she said thoughtfully. "What did you do yesterday?"

With that question, I realized he must not have said much. I tried unsuccessfully to relax.

"We went to the zoo and walked through the park."

She nodded. "Beautiful day for it. The kids were okay for you all by yourself?"

I took a sip of my tea, which was too hot, but I didn't want to answer. She watched me in a way that left me certain she would give me no quarter.

"Charlie came with us."

Her eyes gogged for a fraction of a second, but she smiled. "You're kidding."

I shook my head. "He told me he didn't take the kids out often, but I didn't believe it to be all *that* bad. Is it?"

She shrugged, tilting her head in thought. "He's not the type for fatherly outings, no. Only because he's just so busy—or that's what he says. I suspect there's a bit more to do with it than that though. Charlie has hidden behind his job for as long as I've known him. Being alone is hard enough without the addition of two small children you're not accustomed to caring for. Charlie doesn't even look after himself, and he has a hard time believing that he should be allowed to."

"He told me as much."

Katie quietly assessed me. "I've something to offer, and it doesn't require a response, just something I feel I should say. I hope you'll forgive me for being so bold. It's plain to see something's happening between you two—not only from his face this morning, but in yours right now."

I straightened, my heartbeat doubling up for a breath before finding its rhythm again.

She held up a hand. "No, don't say anything. I'm not asking. I just want you to understand something about Charlie that you might know—or you might not. Charlie has had a rough go of things, and because of that, because he's so deep in his hurt, he makes things more complicated than they have to be. He wants so very badly to be happy, to find a way to be all the things he wishes for. As long as I've had the pleasure of working for Charlie, he carries his past on his shoulders like it's his cross to bear. And ever since you've come into this home, he has found a second wind."

I looked down into my tea, unable to speak.

"I'm not insinuating there's more between you two than there is. I'm only saying that your calm breath in this house has already changed it for the better. It's plain to see from where I'm standing, and I'm certain it is from where Charlie's standing too. There's worry on your face, and I want to tell you not to fret, no matter what's happened or what will happen. Because things always work out. The big wheel turns on and on. The clock ticks without sleeping, and life goes on."

Katie offered a reassuring smile that did its job. She pushed off the counter.

"Well, the laundry won't wash itself, and thank goodness for that. I'd be out of a job."

I laughed, and she headed into the laundry room, leaving me to my thoughts.

It was true, what she'd said. The world turned on, and things kept moving forward. And I'd felt the change in Charlie just as she'd said, humbled and moved at the idea that I had helped him find his way. Because that was what I wanted more than anything—his happiness.

And as for the rest, I would leave it behind me and look ahead, keeping my eyes on the hope that I wouldn't stumble into him again, for my heart's sake.

CHARLIE

My tie had long been loosened by the time I looked up from my computer that night. It was nearly eleven, which didn't surprise me, given the bleary state of my eyes or the steady ache behind them.

To say the day had been long would be a gross understatement.

I'd gotten to work before most everyone—there always seemed to be someone there, the grind unceasing. I'd even managed to tell myself that I'd come in earlier strictly for my desire to get ahead.

Seemed making up lies to tell myself was my favorite pastime.

In all honesty, I hadn't slept much at all, so when I'd woken at five without a single hope of drifting away again, I'd pulled myself out of bed. I'd showered and tried not to think about Hannah's face when I'd walked away from her the night before. I'd shaved and reminded myself I was doing the right thing. I'd dressed and told myself just what a shitty, miserable man I was to have ignored reason for my own wants.

Because in doing that, I'd hurt her. And in hurting her, I'd hurt myself.

It was likely I'd ruined everything in the process.

The subway had been relatively quiet at six in the morning, and

I had been left to my thoughts as the train clicked down the tracks.

Spending the day with her had been too much. The admissions, the wine—it had all been more than I could bear. There should have been a line between us, a boundary, but there was none. I'd singlehandedly erased it with words that were too honest and lips that were too willing.

I wondered if she felt the moment was a mistake. I wondered if she blamed me.

She should.

I'd taken advantage of her. I'd taken advantage of her friendship and kindness, her sweetness and care. I'd placed my burden on her, drawn her into the tangled knot of my life and heart. I'd been talking about my wife, for God's sake. And that wasn't how I wanted to kiss her for the first time.

Because I wanted to. God, how I wanted to.

My mind sounded its warning, and it was right and wrong, just as right and wrong as my heart was.

It was selfish and unfair to her. I couldn't give her what she deserved, what she needed, not as broken down as I was. I couldn't ask her to heal me, to fix me, to bear with me while I sorted through the wreckage of my failed marriage and failed fatherhood. I didn't want to hurt her, and I felt certain I would. Because the truth was that I didn't know myself anymore, and I didn't know how to be what Hannah needed.

I had been alone for so long, I didn't even know the mechanics of dating, or whatever people called it now. The rules had changed since I was last single, and I'd been left in the dust. I hadn't been on a date since Mary left, before that even, long before.

But even with that knowledge, even with all those facts to stack up and nod at and applaud for their rightness, I my heart couldn't find a way to subscribe. Hannah was everything I'd ever been looking for—someone kind, someone who put others above themselves. Someone who smiled, who found joy and beauty in the world.

The opposite of my ex-wife. Wife. *Her.*

Going to a museum or the theater with Mary had been a chore, her constant criticism and boredom maddening. Dinners alone with her had been endured with large quantities of alcohol, but mostly, we had gone out with friends since being alone with each other was generally unbearable. *Mostly* we had been with Jack, sometimes accompanied by his girl of the week.

Looking back made me feel like a fool. They'd been playing cat and mouse with me in the middle, unaware and smiling and unbelievably stupid.

I tried to imagine Hannah doing something like that to me, something manipulative and cruel, and I couldn't. I thought about taking her to a museum and imagined her face turned up to a painting, full of wonder, like she'd had when the zoo clock chimed and the animals danced. I imagined her sweet smile across the table from me while out at dinner and thought I wouldn't need a drop of alcohol to feel completely drunk.

But I circled back around, my mind guiding my heart back to the point. I couldn't have Hannah because I couldn't give her what she needed or what she deserved.

I sighed and pushed back from my desk, packing my bag and clicking off my light. Down the elevator I went and to the curb, hand in the air to hail a cab.

It was late, and I hoped she'd be asleep when I got home. In honesty, it was the reason I'd stayed late. I knew I'd have to answer for what I'd done, but I thought maybe a little time would ease the matter, calm my nerves, bring me answers.

Lies, lies, lies. I'd just keep on telling myself what I wanted to hear. Maybe something would stick.

I laughed to myself. What was one more lie on the pile?

I unlocked the door, praying I'd find the house silent as I stepped in. But luck hadn't been on my side in a long time, and it didn't choose that moment to make the move.

Music floated in from the kitchen, pretty acoustic guitar riffs and the soft voice of a man who'd lost love and lived to tell. When I stepped into the doorway, there Hannah stood.

Her lips moved only a little as she sang along, her long fingers rolling up dough with preserves in the center. Baking supplies littered the island, and a sheet of already rolled pastries sat just next to her workspace. She leaned into the counter, her hips flush against it, body arching just a little, just enough to curve her back. The shadow of her long body was blurred under the gauzy white fabric of her nightgown, her arms bare, fingers covered in flour, blonde hair tumbling down her back in untended waves.

She was magic, quiet and steady and astounding and real, though she felt like something I'd only dreamed.

"I didn't think you'd still be up," I said, wanting to break the moment before I did something stupid.

She jumped and touched her chest, leaving streaks of white flour on her skin. "You startled me."

"I'm sorry." I stepped into the room, heading for a stool so I could sit across from her with the counter between us. It was safer that way.

She flushed, turning her eyes back to her task. "I couldn't sleep."

I nodded. Silence hung between us. I swallowed.

It had to be me. I had to speak. I owed her that.

So I took a breath and did just that. "Hannah, I'm sorry."

She shook her head, her eyes still down as she rolled the dough up. "Please, don't. Let's just not talk about it."

Another swallow, my throat attempting to work that tightness away to no avail. "I have to. I need to tell you …"

Hannah glanced up at me, pain and worry on her brows. "It's all right."

It was just what she'd said to me last night, but tonight, it meant something completely different.

"It's not all right." I scanned her face, her eyes, her lips that had consumed my thoughts since I first saw them smile. "I'm sorry because the timing is wrong. I'm sorry because this—our situation—is so much more complicated than I wish it were. I'm sorry I crossed the line, Hannah. I'm sorry the line's there at all." I ran a hand through my hair, not feeling like I was explaining myself well enough. "I don't even know if that makes sense."

"It does," she said quietly, her hands still and folded in front of her on the counter.

I nodded once, feeling grateful but not knowing what else to say. I was afraid to admit much more. If I cracked the door open further, I'd end up with her in my arms. I knew it as well as I knew my name.

"I wish things were different," she said softly, an unexpected admission, her eyes so open, so honest.

I fought the lump in my throat down again before saying the only thing I could, "Me too."

Hannah sighed, a heavy sound, turning back to her pastries and closing the conversation with grace and ease. "Was your day productive?"

My sigh echoed hers, and I leaned on the island surface. "Productive enough. How are the kids?"

"They're all right. Maven had a fever today and barely ate. I'm going to keep her home tomorrow."

I nodded. "That's fine. She can't go to school with a fever anyway. Is she okay?"

"We'll see how she is in the morning. I gave her ibuprofen, and she went to sleep early. I was going to go up with a cool cup of water and check on her when I finished here."

"I'll do it," I said and stood, heading for the cabinet where her sippy cups were. "What are you making?"

"*Banketstaaf*. It's a pastry roll with almond paste and apricot jam in the middle. We usually make them for *Sinterklaas*, but I had a taste for them."

I twisted off the lid of the plastic cup and filled it up at the fridge. "*Sinterklaas*? Like Santa?"

She chuckled. "Not quite. But Holland is where your Santa came from. When I was a girl, we didn't really celebrate Christmas. *Sinterklaas* comes on his boat from Spain, and for a week before his birthday on the sixth, we leave our wooden shoes out with hay and carrots for his horse."

"Like stockings?"

"Yes, you got the idea for that from us too," she joked. "And, at night on the fifth, the doorbell rings, and there will be a sack of presents on the stoop. Such magic."

I smiled, screwing the lid back on. "I like that."

She smiled back. "I do too. It's a time for family, and our gifts are usually handmade with poems or letters from *Sinterklaas*, but really, we all give them to each other, though the children don't know. The trick is to be the most clever, to have the funniest poem and a gift that matches. Like, once, my oma gave me a rolling pin that had been my great-grandmother's with a poem that told me never to stop doing what I loved or what fulfilled me."

"I think I like your oma. And the holiday sounds like magic, just like you said. I'd like to see that."

"Maybe someday you will."

I caught my mind wandering again, imagining walking the canals of Amsterdam during the holidays with Hannah, and I shook the thought away, turning. "Well, I'll go check on Maven and try to get some sleep."

"All right. I'll finish up here and see you in the morning."

I couldn't help but look back, and I found her watching me leave. And that made it so much harder to go.

But I told myself once more that I was doing the right thing, and I almost believed myself that time.

Almost.

Quite Contrary

HANNAH

The next morning, I woke feeling better than the day before though still unsure in my own way. Thankful as I was for clearing the air with Charlie, to bear the admission that he wished things were different didn't help me let the idea of him go.

But as I'd pulled the pastries from the oven the night before, lost in my own thoughts, I'd refocused my attention to the kids and my job.

That was the only thing I could control, so I found a way to accept the fact.

Charlie was in the kitchen eating that morning, one foot hooked on the rung of his stool, the other long leg stretched out, his eyes on his phone as he read. He glanced up when I passed, and we shared a smile that made me believe things might be all right.

Up the stairs I went, not hearing Maven's cries until I was halfway up, and louder and louder they grew. My nerves climbed too, and when I opened her bedroom door, she nearly broke my heart.

She sat in her bed, face red and wet from crying, the covers bunched up around her. She'd thrown up, leaving evidence in her hair and the bed, down the front of her clothes, and from the smell of her, it wasn't the only sick.

I whispered to her in Dutch and picked her up, not minding my clothes. She was burning up.

I hurried out of her room and called down the stairs for Charlie. He bounded up to meet me two steps at a time, his face tight with concern.

"Will you wake Sammy and get him to school?" I asked. "I think it's best if he's there today."

He brushed Maven's hair back. "She's on fire. Here, let me take her."

I hesitated. "Let me wash her. You can't get sick. Just take care of Sammy, and I'll bring her to see you once she's cleaned up so I can change her bedding."

He nodded, though his eyes didn't leave his daughter. "Katie," he called over his shoulder. Her head appeared around the banister at the foot of the stairs. "Can you help out? Maven's sick."

"Of course," she answered, heading up to us.

I tucked Maven into my chest and rocked her, rubbing her back as she wailed. "Let me go get her bathed."

"Thank you. I'll take care of everything else."

I headed to the bathroom, soothing Maven. She was miserable, couldn't stop crying, so her bath was short. By the time I made it back to her room, Katie had the big curtains pushed back but the sheers still pulled to keep the room a little dark, and Maven's sheets were fresh. I left her in a Pull-Up and grabbed a light blanket to wrap her in, taking her temperature last.

When the ear thermometer beeped, I did the math ... 101 Fahrenheit was 38 Celsius—a solid fever but not unmanageable. After a dose of ibuprofen, I gathered her up and sat in her rocker, soothing and patting her back until she finally stopped crying.

Charlie came in a few minutes after, his face bent with worry and something else as he looked us over, something I didn't have the constitution to consider in the moment.

Maven looked over at him and began to cry again, reaching for him.

He stepped over and picked her up, holding her flush against his chest as her little arms stretched to reach around his neck.

I sighed.

"Maybe I should stay home." He shifted from side to side, rocking her.

"Her fever isn't so high that it's dangerous. You should go to work."

"I don't want to go," he said with his hand on her back and his eyes full of worry.

My heart clenched. "Well, you don't have to, but I think you should. You'll be behind for a week if you don't. I'm here. I'll take care of her, and if she gets worse, I promise I'll let you know so you can come back straightaway."

Charlie drew in a breath and let it out, not seeming to like the arrangement but knowing I was right. "All right."

"We'll get a little food and water in her, and once her medicine kicks in, she'll be fine. Don't worry."

He nodded, his eyes traveling down the front of me. "That makes two shirts my kids have ruined."

My brows quirked, and I looked down to find a little sick down the front of me. "And many more to come, I'm sure. It's fine though. Let me go change."

We traded places, and I paused at the door for a moment at the sight of him sitting in the rocking chair in a suit and tie, rocking his sick daughter with drawn brows and downcast eyes, his cheek pressed against her blonde hair.

And then I sighed again and walked away. Katie, who had occupied Sammy, offered a sympathetic smile as I passed, and I hurried down the stairs to change quickly, hurrying back up to trade places with Charlie once more. When I was seated, he took a long look at Maven, running his hand over her hair.

"Call me if she gets worse, okay?"

"I promise," I said.

And, with a final weary smile, he left.

That afternoon, that promise was fulfilled.

She'd thrown up three more times, unable to keep down water or medicine, and when she woke from a nap, her fever had climbed until it was out of control at 104.

Katie shook her head at the thermometer as I rocked a lethargic Maven in my arms. "It's after four — too late to call the pediatrician. You've got to take her to the emergency room."

"I think so too," I said grimly.

Her face pinched in thought. "The closest is Mount Sinai. You know, Mary works there. But I just don't know if it's worth going to another hospital. Maybe she'll actually be there and find a way to be present for her child, for once," she added with disdain.

I tried not to consider any of that, my thoughts focused on Maven alone.

"I'll call Charlie and a cab," Katie said, "and I'll get her bag and insurance card together. You go get her into some pajamas."

I nodded and hurried to get her dressed and grab her freshly washed bunny and blanket, rushing back down. Katie took her—I tried to ignore the chill of my damp sweater where she'd been curled against my chest—and I put on my shoes and coat, grabbing my wallet from my bag and stuffing it into the diaper bag. And with a kiss on the cheek from Katie, we were out the door.

I didn't check my phone until we were in the cab. A text from Charlie waited, saying he'd meet us there. Katie would get Sammy from school.

Everything would be fine. Maven would be fine.

Kids get fevers all the time, I told myself. But it didn't stop me from being scared.

The waiting room wasn't very full, and before long, we were taken back to first get her temperature and weight and then to a small room where we were told to wait again. So I climbed in the big hospital bed with her and held her.

I sang to her in Dutch until her breathing slowed. The occasional twitch of her arms or hands told me she was well asleep, but I kept singing anyway, as if to chase away the ghosts and the fear and the quiet of the cold, sterile room. And I watched the little square window on the door, waiting to see Charlie's face.

When I did, it was wild with worry, and I made a *shh* shape with my lips, hoping he would understand. He did, gently opening the door and quietly closing it behind him. She didn't stir.

His tie was loose and shirt rumpled, his coat and jacket and bag abandoned in the stiff chair next to the bed, but his eyes never left Maven as he sat on the edge, his body brushing my legs, his hand reaching for her back. I shifted, leaning forward to hand her off, but he shook his head and smiled. It was a tired smile, a sad smile.

I hadn't stopped singing.

It was ten or fifteen minutes before a doctor came in, making no effort to be quiet, not that Maven would have been able to sleep anyway once the poking and prodding began. She woke up crying, and after a bit of inspection and some questions, it was decided that they'd administer an IV, give her some antinausea medicine, and monitor her for a few hours.

The doctor blew out, and in blew a nurse with supplies.

The IV was the worst part of the whole ordeal.

I tried to pass her off to Charlie again, but she clung to me and screamed, "Nana"—her version of my name—so I held her still, singing to her with my voice trembling.

Charlie held her face to stay her eyes as the nurse pricked her arm. Her cry broke my heart.

The nurse smiled apologetically and when it was done, she gathered her things, handing off a popsicle that would hopefully stop Maven's stomach from emptying again. And then she dimmed the lights and passed us the television remote.

Charlie found some cartoons, and Maven sat cradled in my lap, slowly eating the popsicle but eating it all the same. That at least was a comfort. Charlie stayed on the edge of the bed, and though I kept trying to pass her over, he just refused, seeming content just to watch us.

Watch her, I reminded myself.

But his eyes would find mine over and over again, his hand and body close enough to my thigh that we touched, the warmth of him radiating into me in the chill of the room.

When Maven's popsicle was gone and she fell asleep again, he stood and leaned over, pressing his lips to my ear. "I'm gonna get coffee. Want one?"

His whispering breath sent a shudder down my spine.

I nodded.

His hand covered mine that covered Maven's, and when he stood, he smiled at me with gratitude. And then he left the room, taking my resolve with him.

It was impossible. Being around him, working for him, pretending I didn't want him, pretending like I didn't notice that he wanted me too—all of it.

Being professional was a pipe dream. My heart had already moved over the line, and there would be no going back.

I found myself truly wondering what was stopping us, what stood in between us. There was nothing in my contract with Charlie or the agency that forbade it, not aloud, only an unspoken expectation.

But most of the men au pairs worked for were married, and Charlie wasn't, not in the way that mattered. He was older, yes, but not so much that I noticed the fact.

Of course, if things didn't work out—and the truth was that they probably wouldn't, a truth that was only a whisper I did little to acknowledge—my job would be affected. I would probably have to leave, not only Charlie and the children, but America. Because I very much doubted the agency would place me a third time.

But going home wouldn't hurt so badly if I lost what I'd found. In fact, if I lost the life I'd built here, home was the only place I'd want to be.

The truth in my heart was that I wanted Charlie, and if he wanted me too, it was worth the risk. If he would only say yes, we could both have what we wanted.

I only had to find the courage to ask.

CHARLIE

I headed out into the hospital hallway with a shortness of breath and a muddled brain, making my way toward the coffee vending machines I'd seen back in the waiting area.

Regret pressed on me for going to work. I would rather have been behind than not have been there for my baby. I'd worried over her all day, and when I'd looked in the window of the hospital room, the guilt had been more than I could bear.

The sight of Maven so sick made me ache all over.

The sight of Hannah holding Maven when she was so sick made me ache just in the rib cage.

She'd been singing softly in Dutch when I walked in, holding my daughter with tenderness and care I'd never seen from Maven's own mother. The thought had cut me, cut me so deeply I didn't know if the wound would ever heal.

The war of what I'd known with Mary versus what I'd seen in Hannah pulled and tugged at my thoughts. How had I not seen how bad it was all those years? How had I not realized? How hadn't I known what the kids were missing, what I was missing?

But then I admitted to myself that I had known. I'd known all along, forever. And I'd done nothing about it.

And that was the worst part of all.

I stepped up to the coffee machine and fed it my money, watching it pour sludge into the cup that we would hold to warm our hands and little more. I wished I had something more to give her than the burned goo, like a cup of tea on fine china or an espresso or *something* good. She deserved something good.

She deserved so much.

And I had nothing to offer.

She deserved someone without baggage, without history she'd have to take on for her own. She deserved someone as fresh and pure and beautiful as her.

I was none of those things.

And still, I wanted her, and she wanted me too. I could see it plainly in her face, in the blue of her irises, at the edge of her lips, in the corners of her eyes. There was a light in her that flared a little brighter when I came near.

I could see it. And I shouldn't have wanted to do anything about it, but I did.

As the sludge steamed and poured, I wished I'd met her somewhere, anywhere else. If only things were simpler … even a *little* simpler would have been enough.

I shook my head as I took the cup once the machine stopped sputtering and started it again.

Get it together, Charlie.

She felt right, so right, but somehow *wrong* too. No, not wrong ... not in the sense of her and me, but like I was supposed to *think* it was wrong. Because of some outside force, from the expectation hanging over us. Over me. But the truth of the matter was that Hannah felt right in all the ways that counted, and fighting that feeling was exhausting.

When the second cup was finished, I picked it up, chancing a sip of mine. I made a face when the brackish muck hit my tongue, certain it would keep me up and partly convinced it was radioactive.

I turned down the hallway, so lost in thought that I didn't see *her* until I was almost at the door. I stopped dead, heart included.

Mary stood outside the door, peering into the window at an angle. Dark circles lay nestled under her eyes, her dark hair in a tight ponytail, her dark eyes trained into the room where our feverish daughter lay.

"Who is she?" She didn't look at me.

"The nanny," I said stupidly.

"She's pretty." There was an edge to her voice, but it was dull.

I watched her for a series of thudding heartbeats before I spoke. "Where the fuck have you been, Mary?"

"Here," she said hollowly, never moving besides her lips.

"That's cute. I suppose the divorce papers got lost in the mail and you dropped your cell phone on the subway track. Does that sound about right?"

"I don't know what you want from me, Charlie—"

"Are you serious? Are you fucking *serious* right now?" I hissed, trying not to yell, the thick coffee rippling in the cups from my shaking hands. I took a breath. "No. You know what? I'm not having that argument with you. Here's the truth: All I want from you is one thing."

She finally turned and met my gaze, hers empty, mine on fire—I could feel it boiling deep down in my guts, steaming up my throat.

"Let us go. Sign a waiver and let us go once and for all."

She pushed off the wall and turned to leave.

"Goddammit, Mary, don't you walk away from me. You've done that enough."

"I can't give you what you want, Charlie. Not now, not ever."

"What the hell does that even mean? I mean, you're right about the fact that you can't give me love or companionship or even a goddamn divorce. I've even had to do that alone. But do you intend to keep me firmly placed in hell until you get the fucking notion? Because that's where you've left me."

She shrugged and tried to turn away again.

My rage almost boiled over, but I swallowed it, pushed it down, sucked in a breath. Because our child was sick, and Mary was here even if only out of obligation. Maven needed her, and that had to be all that mattered.

"Stop. I'll stop. Just … just come in and see her."

Mary shook her head and kept turning, her eyes on the ground and the line of her profile in my eyeline. "I can't. I'm sorry."

"You're not fucking sorry," I shot at her back. "You're her mother. Her *mother*. And if you were really sorry, if you gave a fuck about anybody but yourself, you would go in there and be her mother."

But she said nothing, just kept walking, and I had no desire to stop her. She'd disappointed me for years, and now was no exception, only a reminder.

Somehow, the cups still hung in the circles of my hands, not crushed with its contents spilling over my fingers, not flying through the air in the direction she walked. And I stood there, staring at her back, helpless and hopeless.

Until I walked up to the door and looked through the window at Hannah and Maven, asleep in each other's arms.

She was everything Mary wasn't. They were day and night, the angel and the devil. And I knew I would find salvation in Hannah's arms just as I'd found hell in Mary's.

In that moment, I'd never been so certain of anything in my life.

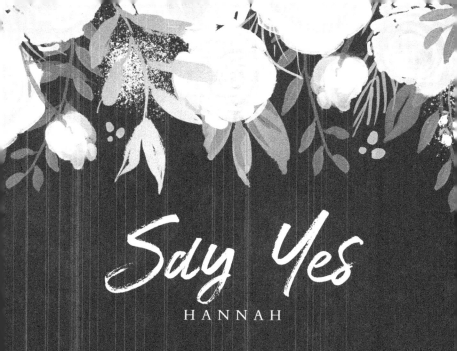

Say Yes

HANNAH

When I woke, Maven was still breathing slowly, her face soft with sleep and cheeks rosy with fever. Charlie sat in the chair against the wall, leg crossed ankle to knee, his eyes on his untouched coffee.

He looked up, and we shared a smile, nothing more. We could blame the silence on Maven, but it was more than that. We were lost in thought, content with not speaking because there seemed to be too much to say and no way to say it.

Maven finally stirred, and we were able to get her to eat a cracker and drink some water. And once it was clear she would keep it down, they let us leave, though not before arming us with more magical popsicles and instructions to bring her back if she got worse or didn't show signs of improvement.

Charlie was turned inward, his eyes distant as he held Maven in the taxi, his hand on her back, his head bowed and cheek resting against her crown. I watched him without watching, felt him without action or words. The tension was unbearable, our worry over Maven paramount. The stress of hospitals and poking and prodding and concern had left its mark on both of us. We were tired. For so many reasons, we were tired.

It was late by the time we made it home, and we shuffled in to find a very worried Katie. Charlie carried Maven upstairs to put her to bed, and I told Katie what had happened. When Charlie came down, Katie was pulling on her coat, and within a few minutes, she was gone, the door closing behind her, leaving me alone with Charlie and the silence.

With nothing left to be done and no more tasks to occupy my mind, emotions surged, welling in my chest, pricking my eyes and stinging my nose. I dropped onto the bench and folded in on myself, resting my face in my palms to hide my tears.

"Hey," he said softly, moving to kneel in front of me. He touched the outside of my knee, the weight of his hand a comfort and a curse.

I moved my hands and met his eyes, swiping at my cheeks, laughing around a sob at the absurdity of it all.

"I'm sorry. I don't know why I'm crying. It was only a fever, and she's fine, but ..." I looked down at my hands, drawing in a breath and letting it go in an effort to stave off more tears. "It was hard to endure all the same. Scary." I shook my head and said again, "I'm sorry. It's so silly."

"No, it's not," he said quietly, his face mirroring my heart. "I don't think it's silly at all. To not be able to help someone you love when they're hurting is a desolate, powerless thing."

I nodded, hands in my lap, his eyes on mine, so deep and dark. "That was how I felt. Helpless. But there was no real danger. I shouldn't be upset. I should be ..." *Braver, stronger, better, more.*

His hand shifted from my knee to clasp my fingers. "Hannah,

you're allowed to feel how you feel."

The meaning was double, I knew. I could feel it in the place where our hands touched, in the timbre of his voice, in the velvety depths of his eyes.

My lungs sipped quick and shallow, but there wasn't enough air. "Is it that simple?"

"I want to believe it is."

Our faces were angled to each other—mine down, his up. He reached for my face, cupped my cheek, warming the cold tracks of my tears with his palm, giving me courage.

I didn't want him to disappear again. I didn't want him to say *no* again.

And I found my voice, the words summoned from the quiet of my heart, and I parted my lips to speak. "Say yes, Charlie. Tell me you want me." I wasn't sure I'd said it aloud; my thundering heart was all I could hear.

"I've wanted you since you walked through the door," he said without hesitation. "I've wanted you since I first saw you smile."

I leaned in, and so did he.

"Say yes," I whispered against his lips, the nerves in mine tingling.

"Yes," he begged the answer, begged my heart.

I closed the inches with the slightest of movements and pressed my aching lips to his.

A burst of awareness shot through me, a complete focus of the place where our lips touched, soft and relieved and fevered. I leaned into his palm as his hands held my face, as if I were precious, guiding me to the angle he desired. His tongue swept my lips for passage, and I granted it, opening to let him in. His shirt was crisp under my fingers as they roamed up to his neck, to his jaw, holding him close, begging him not to stop, not to think, not to disappear, not to do what was right.

I leaned too far, tipping his balance, but the kiss didn't stop —

he stood, taking me with him by way of his hands on my face. No, the kiss didn't stop at all; it deepened the moment the length of our bodies pressed against each other, the sound of our breath in my ears, the feel of his hot mouth on mine possessing every thought.

When he broke away, it wasn't with fear or regret; it was with tenderness. It was with his forehead pressed to mine and lips still close but not close enough.

"I don't want to stop," he whispered.

"Then don't," I whispered back and kissed away his doubt and my own.

I lost myself in him for a long while, in the feeling of his lips and hands, in the sensation of his body against mine, my arms around his neck, squeezing to hold him close, closer still. The deeper the kiss went, the hotter it burned. The more I wanted him, the more urgent I felt.

With everything I had, I stopped, breath ragged, heart hammering, needing air, needing him.

"Charlie," I breathed.

He touched my face, trailing his fingers along the line of my jaw. "Hannah …"

I closed my eyes at the fire on his fingertips. And when I opened them, there was only one thing to do.

"Come with me," I said, my voice quiet.

I took Charlie's hand in mine, and he followed me to the stairs that led down to my room. But when my hand touched the rail, he pulled me to a stop.

I turned to him, a jolt of fear pulsing through me at the thought that it was over, that it would end now, that he'd say a word and I'd be banished again.

I didn't speak; I couldn't.

"Hannah," he said, searching my face, "we don't have to do this."

The fear surged, closing my throat and speeding my heart.

He regrets me already. He only wants me for a moment, for tonight. He doesn't want me at all.

"You don't want …" I tripped over my thoughts. "I thought you said …"

He stepped into me, quieting my worry with his lips, strong and sure against mine. It was a kiss that told me how much he *did* want, a kiss that soothed and eased and relieved my fear, replacing it with certainty.

He broke away and looked into my eyes. "I meant what I said. And all I want to do is follow you down those stairs. But I don't want you to … I don't want you to regret this, regret me. I want you to be sure."

And with my worries put away, I smiled and said, "Oh, I'm sure."

I held his hand and towed him down the stairs in a hurry, and he followed.

When we reached my dark room, I let him go, moving to the lamp next to my bed. With a click, there was light, just a little, just enough to see the look on his face when I turned.

Worry and want creased his brow, tightened the corners of his eyes, but he wasn't second-guessing me or us—that I knew. He seemed unsure of himself, and I realized something I hadn't considered before.

Charlie had been married for years, alone for months, and though he could have been with another woman since he'd been alone, his face, his body, told me that he hadn't.

I stepped into him slowly, threading my fingers through his, my eyes on his and his on mine.

"Are you afraid?" I asked softly.

He touched my face again, gently brushing my hair back. "I don't know what I'm doing, Hannah."

I moved his hand in mine to my waist and left it there, skating my hands up his chest, angling my lips to his. "Yes, you do," I said simply.

And I kissed him to prove it.

He kissed me back, and his lips knew just what to do as they parted. His hands knew what to do as they roamed up the back of my sweater, hot against my bare skin. His body knew what to do, winding around mine as mine wound around his.

But still he was hesitant, not pressing for more, not taking what I knew he wanted.

So I took it instead.

My hands found his shirt buttons—the kiss went on and on, blissfully unrelenting—and I unfastened them from top to bottom, tugging the tail of his shirt from his pants, sliding it over his shoulders, down his arms. My determined fingers reached for the hem of my sweater and broke that never-ending kiss for only long enough to pull it off and toss it away.

It wasn't until I unfastened his belt that he awoke, that his hands followed the lead of my own, moving from face to neck to breast. He cupped the swell, his kiss deeper for a moment, harder, searching my mouth, searching deeper when I reached into his pants, finding his long, hard length hot and pent.

He moaned into my mouth at the touch. I freed him, stroked him, gripped him until his hips flexed and his arms wound around me, pulling me into him, telling me he wanted me. He wanted me soon, and he wanted me fast.

We kissed as he stepped me backward to the bed, steadying me as he laid me down, pressing me into the bed with his body for a long moment before he broke away.

Down my neck his lips moved, closing over my skin with a sweep of his tongue until they reached the valley between my breasts. My fingers wound through his golden hair, my heart thudding against his lips, as his fingers hooked in the edge of my bra to pull, baring me to him, to his warm, wet mouth, to his tongue that swept the peak of my nipple. His hand roamed while his mouth was busy, deftly unbuttoning my pants before slipping inside, into my panties, cupping the heat of me, his fingertips tracing the line of my core.

His teeth grazed my nipple at the same moment he slipped a finger into me, gently curling it, squeezing his palm.

I gasped his name, bucked my hips.

I was helpless as his hand flexed and his lips moved and his breath puffed hot and loud against my breast. It wasn't until he lost his patience with my clothes that he backed away, and I was able to think. His purpose was to rid me of my pants and panties, a hurried tugging that gave me time to reach behind me and unclasp my bra. And when I looked up at him, his eyes were dark, running up and down my body that lay stretched out on the bed.

With elegant grace, he stood, pushing his pants down his legs, and once he stepped out of them, he hooked the backs of my knees and pulled, dragging me to the end of the bed with enough force to surprise me. And then he knelt reverently at the foot of the bed and spread my thighs, his eyes locked where my legs met, his lips slightly open, his hands searching, fingers parting me, mouth descending.

His heat met mine, a silky wet sweeping of his tongue against the aching center of me.

Charlie knew what to do. He knew exactly what to do.

My lungs filled with a gasp so deep, it burned, and I held the air there, held it because I couldn't move. Only my heart took action, galloping in my ribs, faster and harder with every spurring of his tongue and slip of his fingers into me, out of me, into me again.

His name passing my lips in a whispered moan sent a rumble from his throat and into my center. A hiss through my teeth followed when my core flexed, throbbing around his finger.

His mouth moved over my thigh, across my stomach, his fingers still working me, still moving as he climbed up my body, not stopping until he was at my lips. I kissed him like I'd been starving for him, with desperation and desire, the tang of my body on his lips sending me over the edge, my mouth opening wider, tongue deeper, wanting more.

The bare length of him pressed against me, and at the contact, he broke away, panting.

"I don't ..." he breathed, seeming not to have the mind to finish the thought other than one word. *"Condom."*

"You're safe?" I asked.

He nodded.

"I'm safe—on birth control. Trust you," I whispered the truth in truncated sentences, not wanting anything but him inside me.

He kissed me deep but pulled back again to ask, "Sure?"

I nodded and pulled him down onto me.

Everything was heavy—my body, his body, our breath, our heartbeats and hands. He pushed my thighs open with his knees, settling between them, the tip of him at the edge of me. I angled for him, spreading my legs, begging with my body.

He flexed his hips and gave me what I'd asked for with aching slowness.

And we breathed. For a long moment, we breathed and felt and didn't move other than a pulse of his cock that my core echoed around him.

And then he kissed me.

He kissed me with abandon, with worship and desire, and as his lips told me what words couldn't, he moved, pumping his hips, rolling them when he hit the end, a wave that filled and pressed and gave my body what it wanted, what it needed. Awareness slipped away. There was only the point where our bodies joined, the nerves in my body firing. Harder he pushed—he was close; I could feel it in his body, I could hear it on his breath. And with a thrust, a low rumble in his throat, my name, a whisper, he came, pulsing inside me, the release of his body too much as he hit me fast and deep.

And I lost control, my body squeezing once and letting go in succession, drawing him deeper into me, thighs holding him, my hips rocking, rocking, slower as it faded away, leaving my body sensitive and sated.

He kissed me, kissed me with care and adoration and a sweet, lingering softness. When he backed away, he smoothed my hair, scanned my face, met my eyes. And I found I only wanted one thing in the world.

"Stay," I whispered.

Charlie kissed me again and did just that.

Dreaming is Free
CHARLIE

Awareness crept over me, a slow waking of my mind, marking the sensations that were so foreign to me—Hannah's legs scissored with mine, her head tucked under my chin, the softness of her breath against my skin, her arms tucked between us. I held her tighter, drew her closer, eyes still closed.

There were very few times in my life when I'd woken tangled up in someone else—mostly in college, before Mary. She and I always seemed to come together and part ways at the first opportunity, and we *never* touched when we slept. But Hannah and I'd found each other in the dark; even when we'd shifted or rolled over, the other would move to keep the connection.

I found it incredible that so much had changed over the course of one night.

The second I had knelt in front of her as she cried, I should have known there would be no going back. And I didn't want to. I only wished I'd taken the leap long before.

For a moment, everything had hung in the balance, all the balls in the air, the uncertainty between us almost oppressive. But then she'd asked me to say yes, and I'd given her what she wanted. I'd wanted the same thing all along.

I'd wondered for a moment as I held her tear-stained cheek if she wanted me the way I wanted her. I'd wondered if it was real, if it was Hannah who made me feel this way or if we were a product of the situation, of the environment.

But when we'd kissed, I'd had no doubt that it was *her*. It was Hannah. It was the sweetness of her, the kindness, the gentleness of her that called to me. It was her smile and her laugh and the joy she made me feel. It was the smell of her, like vanilla and cream. It was her eyes, the color of the blue dahlias she'd brought home and displayed in the kitchen.

Hannah was everywhere. In my home. In my heart. In my arms.

Contentment and peace settled over me. I pressed a thankful kiss into her hair.

I'd been so nervous, nearly frozen in uncertainty of how to *be* with her, with what I was supposed to do. It was like it had been the first time all over again, like I was sixteen, nervous and fumbling. And she had known. She had known, and she'd reminded me that I knew what to do after all. I knew very well.

Being with one person for so long had left my other experiences far behind me, and I'd found myself in absolute wonder of Hannah, of her long body, of the taste of her, of the sounds she made and the softness of her. She gave and gave, and I gave right back. There was no taking, no force, just an exchange of adoration that had filled me up, satisfying so much more than my body.

She woke with a long, deep breath through her nose and the shifting of her body to somehow twine even more with mine.

"Mmm," she hummed and kissed me just under my collarbone.

"Morning," I said.

She sighed.

I sighed.

And we lay there together for a few minutes, thinking, my hand skating up and down her bare back, Hannah nestled in my chest.

I wanted to speak, but I wasn't sure what to say. We needed to talk, and I didn't want to. I wanted to stay there in that moment indefinitely, avoiding all responsibility and decision.

"Do you have much work to do today?" she asked, the words puffing against my skin.

"Probably, but I'm not going to do it."

She pulled back, and I looked over her face, younger and more innocent than the picture in my mind.

"No? Even though you left early yesterday? I thought you might work all weekend."

I shrugged a shoulder and smoothed her golden hair. "No, not after yesterday. I shouldn't have gone to work at all, and today I'll make up for that. I want to be here with her. With you."

Her eyes smiled, sparkling and blue and crisp. "I didn't realize it was so easy for you to get away," she teased.

"Well, my priorities have changed." I held her body to mine, gazing upon her face.

"Have they?"

I nodded. "They have. I want to be here as much as I can, more than I'm able. I want more days like the zoo. I ... I want to feel like that again, but I can't if I'm always gone. So, yes. My priorities have changed, my heart has changed, and my *life* has changed, all thanks to you showing me the way."

When she smiled, it was shy and sweet and beautiful. I kissed her; it seemed the only thing to do.

Her long fingers held my jaw, her body arching into mine for the duration.

We watched each other across the pillow, her eyes slipping into uncertainty.

"Charlie, what do we do now?" The question was gentle, and I knew she didn't want to talk about it any more than I did.

"Well," I started, "I'd like to stay here in bed with you until I have no choice but to leave. Then, I'd like to spend the day with you and the kids. And tonight, I'd like to be right here with you again. And tomorrow night. And the night after."

She laughed quietly, smiling like she thought I was patronizing her.

But I didn't laugh. I looked into her eyes so she knew how serious I was.

"Hannah, I don't know what I have to offer you when you've given me so much. And I don't know what will happen from here. I … I haven't done this in a very long time. My head has been telling me that I'm not ready, that I'll hurt you, and I don't want to hurt you." I held her face, brushed her skin with my thumb, breathed through the ache in my chest.

She covered my hand with hers. "Just be honest with me. I'm not fragile; I won't break."

"I have baggage."

"So does everyone. I understand that you've been hurt and why you feel like you're not ready. And with me living here, there's no escape, no separation. I'm worried it will be too much, too fast. Because I can't tell you no, Charlie. I can't pretend I don't want you here as much as I can have you. It's dangerous … you must understand, don't you?"

"I do."

"And so the only way we can do this is if we trust each other. We have to understand that this could easily end whether we want it to or not.

And if it does, when it does, we'll have to deal with the consequences."

"The consequences weren't enough to stop me last night, and they're not enough to stop me now."

She smiled. "They're not enough to stop me either, but that doesn't mean they're not still there."

I watched her for a breath. "It's been a long time since I've trusted anyone. But I trust you."

"Then we'll try," she said. "And what about the children? I don't think we should tell them."

"No, I don't either. But Maven is too young to understand, and I think as long as we're not overly affectionate, Sammy won't think anything of it. I think it's alright to just be what we are—you're already a part of our lives, of their lives. I'm not worried."

She smiled. "Then I won't worry either."

And then I kissed her.

It was slow and gentle, a savoring motion of lips and tongues and hands that roamed. The weight of her breast in my palm, the feel of her thigh between mine, her body flush against me. Every second and every minute with her was a dream, a discovery—not only of her, but of myself.

We would try. I would have her, and she would have me. And the exaltation of that decision brought our bodies together with an easy grace, a long appreciation of each other that went on and on until we were spent and satisfied.

Even then, neither of us wanted to leave the bed or the room or the quiet sanctuary of the morning. But when Maven woke, singing through the baby monitor, our time was up.

Hannah dressed, and I pulled on my slacks, gathering the rest of my clothes before kissing her well and thoroughly at her door. We split up—she headed for the bathroom, and I made my way upstairs, passing Katie in the kitchen. She froze when she saw me, her mouth opening as one brow climbed, her lips stretching into a smile that I returned along with a shrug.

"About time, Charlie," she said.

"You're a terrible influence," I said back and climbed the stairs, still smiling. I might actually smile until I died;, I was so happy.

I tossed my clothes in the direction of my bedroom door and entered Maven's rom, finding her sitting in her bed, singing to her bunny as she made it dance.

"Hey, baby," I cooed as I approached.

She smiled at me. "Daddy!"

I picked her up and propped her on my hip, leaning back to look at her. "Feel better?"

She nodded and hooked her finger in her lips.

"Hungry?"

Another nod.

I kissed her temple. "Come on then."

"*Kai* have a *pa-ka-sickle*?"

I chuckled. "Sure, a medicine popsicle and some toast. What do you say?"

Her answer was to curl into my chest, tucking her head under my neck, a spot where she fit perfectly. For a little while longer at least.

We swung by my room so I could change into jersey pants and a T-shirt before heading downstairs again and into the kitchen. Hannah hadn't come up, and Katie looked like she was about to burst.

She practically bum-rushed me with a fool grin on her face.

I had to laugh as I put Maven in her seat. "Don't try to hide it, Katie."

She giggled—my fifty-something cook actually giggled like a girl—hands clasped in front of her. "I can't help it. I love her, Charlie, and I love you. And the two of you together is just the best. She makes you happy, and you deserve to be happy after all *that woman* put you through."

"You've been a real pro at keeping that under wraps, let me tell you."

She swatted my arm. "Everything's okay, right? That wasn't just a … a one-time thing?"

"I sure hope not."

She giggled again, her cheeks high and pink as she flitted away.

A moment later, Hannah walked in, hair in a long braid over her shoulder and her face full of sunshine.

"Good morning," she said, catching my eyes and holding them as I handed Maven her popsicle.

"Morning," Katie and I echoed.

Hannah took one look at Katie and looked back to me, smiling. "She knows?"

"I think she's been waiting for it for weeks."

Katie and Hannah laughed, but Katie didn't make a fuss.

"Don't worry about me," she said as she turned on the kettle. "I won't make it weird, but you certainly don't have to sneak around me."

"Good," I said. "Come here, Hannah. Let's make out."

They laughed again, but I held out my hand and motioned her over.

"Seriously, come here. Let's show Katie what we're made of."

Hannah's cheeks flushed, shaking her head as she stepped over, took my hand, and kissed me on the cheek before moving away to help Katie with breakfast.

"Ugh, lame," I joked and sat next to Maven, happy as a bunny in a field of clover, feeling blissfully right for the first time in as long as I could remember.

HANNAH

A few hours later, the four of us sat on the couch watching an animated movie. Well, Charlie and I sat close enough that we touched shoulder to hip to knee, and Maven sat in my lap, but Sammy couldn't sit still. At that moment, he was sliding across the coffee table on his belly, face turned to the television. Charlie's eyes were on the papers in his lap—his attempt at working—but when Sammy spun on his stomach and went across the table the way he'd come, Charlie looked up.

"You bored, bud?" he asked.

"*Yesssss*," he hissed. "I'm a snake! *Ik ben de slang!*"

Charlie smiled. "Man, he's picking that up fast."

"*Ja, hij is jong*. He's young and clever and curious."

"Well, I'm doomed then."

I laughed. "*Je kunt leren.*"

One brow rose. "That sounds a little dirty."

"You can learn," I said with my schoolteacher voice. "*Juf* Hannah will teach you."

His smile rose on one side. "Oh, I'm sure *Juf* Hannah could definitely teach me a thing or two."

I chuckled, but he brought the back of his hand to the back of mine, and we threaded our fingers backward together with a squeeze.

"Come on," Charlie said and moved to get up, tossing his paperwork on the coffee table. "Let's go for a walk."

Sammy crowed and jumped through the living room. "A walk, a walk, a walk!"

Charlie ruffled his hair. "Yeah, get some of that energy out. We'll have lunch after. What do you say?"

"Let's *goooooo!*" The word trailed away as he bolted out of the room and to the bench where his shoes were.

Charlie took Maven and felt her forehead. "I think her fever's almost gone. Think we can take her on a walk in the stroller?"

"She's so much better. I think the fresh air might do her good, yeah?"

"*Ja*," he said, smiling as he turned to follow Sammy.

We busied ourselves with shoes and jackets and the stroller, saying goodbye to Katie on our way out into the crisp autumn day.

Charlie held Sammy's hand as we walked toward the park, and I followed with the stroller, watching the two of them talk, Charlie smiling as he looked down at his son, who hadn't stopped talking since we stepped outside.

The sky was high and cloudless and blue, broken only by the fiery tops of the trees as they began their slumber toward spring. The breeze had just the slightest chill, sweeping leaves away in its currents, whispering with their dry crackling against the pavement that the holidays were coming, that scarves and fires and hot chocolate and cinnamon were around the corner.

My eyes traced the treetops that lined the avenue in matching height, marveling over the rusty shade against the cornflower blue of the sky behind them.

"What a lovely day," I said when Sammy began humming.

Charlie glanced over our surroundings, up the street of brownstones with their old iron lamps. "It really is. New York in fall is almost as impressive as New York in spring."

I sighed, smiling. "I would like to see that."

"You will," he said, smiling back. "The park is full of blossoming trees, the grass so green and lush, and everyone is just ... *fresh*. New. Ready for change."

"I can imagine."

He chuckled to himself and rubbed the back of his neck. "Seems like a pretty stupid comparison, thinking about it. Holland is the land of flowers, isn't it?"

"It's true; there are quite a lot of flowers. Tulip fields in spring paint the earth in stripes of color. The grass is always green, even in the winter, and lavender grows everywhere. And autumn is lovely, too. The canals are lined with auburn trees against the old houses. It's a riot of color—green and lush in the summer, gold and warm in the fall. Winter is drab—there's always a bit of rain—but when it snows …" I sighed.

"Do you miss it?"

I shrugged. "Less lately."

He smiled at that, a smile meant only for me. "Good."

We turned the corner for the park, and Charlie stopped at a shop window to look inside.

"Oh, man … the old sandwich shop moved." Disappointment hung on his words. "I loved this place. What a great space. Come here and look."

I stopped the stroller next to the window and peered inside. It was a beautiful shop, long and narrow with big windows, but it was a bit outdated and a little run-down. It had been mostly stripped down, and the sign in the window directed viewers to their new location.

"You should turn this into a bakery," he said.

I laughed genuinely at the suggestion.

But he turned to me, serious. "I mean it. Look, it's already set up and ready to go." He glanced back through the window. "With a little remodeling and some TLC, this place could really be something."

This time when I laughed, I shook my head. "It's a lovely shop, Charlie."

The expression on his face might almost be a pout. "Oh, come on. You can't even daydream about it?"

I looked into the shop again, opening my mouth to speak, but for a second, I said nothing. "I wouldn't even know where to begin. I don't know anything about the business side of things even if I did have the money to rent a space like *this*." I nodded in.

"Psh. You don't need any of those things to dream." He took my hand, gazing in. "What would you do in there? How would you want it to look? Just imagine it, that's all. Dreaming's free."

I sighed and scanned the space, going along with it. "Well, let's see. Pretty new wood floors would make a difference. Open white shelves behind the counter. How high do you think the ceilings are?"

He narrowed his eyes. "Tall. Maybe eighteen feet?"

I nodded, excitement slipping through me as my imagination skipped away from me. "Grand molding. A big chalkboard sign. Cases of pastries with little handwritten signs. Chairs lined up facing out to the street, with a deep table, so you could work here or sit with your friends and look out. A pretty *baldakijn*—how do you say ... a canopy with broad pink-and-white stripes."

He was watching me with his face full of adoration. "See? Dreaming is free. What would you name it?"

"*Lekker*," I answered with a smile as warm as my heart. "It means yummy, delicious. In Dutch, everything is *lekker*." I leaned closer and whispered, "Even bottoms."

Charlie laughed, his head tipping back just a little. He whispered back, eyes twinkling, "How do you say nice butt?"

"*Lekker cont.*"

"Man, that really *does* sound filthy."

I shrugged, and we laughed together and turned back to the sidewalk, hand in hand and smiling. Because he was right; dreaming was free. And I found myself with more dreams every day.

CHARLIE

Central Park was picturesque that day, and so was my life. It was one of those perfect afternoons, the kind you imagined when you were young enough to still believe things would turn out like you thought they would. It was the sound of Sammy laughing as I chased him around a patch of the park and the sight of Hannah sitting on a blanket with Maven in her lap, watching and smiling. It almost felt like déjà vu, a recognition from somewhere deep and elemental that made me believe with some certainty that I was exactly where I was supposed to be. That everything I had been through brought me to that day, to that moment, to the moments after.

And there were so many. Laughing with Katie in the kitchen and eating dinner with Hannah and the kids, getting them ready for bed together—again a natural dance that Hannah and I found ourselves in without need for discussion or instruction, just the two of us moving in synchronicity until both kids were in bed.

We headed downstairs to her room, hand in hand, not ever agreeing to it aloud. It just seemed the only place to go. She'd kept the fireplace clean, and I'd made sure there were an abundance of supplies, so I built a fire while she pulled pillows down, resting them against the footboard.

I lit the lazy log and piled wood on top, and before long, I was sitting with her tucked into my side and her head resting in the curve of my neck, our legs stretched out in front of us and faces turned to the fire as it licked the logs, crackling and popping.

She sighed.

So did I.

"I really don't want to work on Monday," I said regretfully, watching the fire. "Today was too good, and I bet tomorrow will be even better. I'm ruined."

Hannah chuckled. "I can't imagine working as much as you do."

"It's like I'm caught in a wheel that won't stop turning. There's no way to stop it, no way out. I guess it would be different if I loved it, but I don't."

"Did you ever?"

I thought back, searching through those first years. "You know, at first, I think I did. It was exciting, new. I felt like I was contributing, that I was a part of something. About a year in, that was all gone."

"What do you think changed?" she asked.

"I was exhausted," I answered. "It's not sustainable to work that many hours day after day, month after month. Promotions help, and raises make it easier for a minute, but in the end, we're chasing something we can never catch. Because the second one job is over, there are three more to be done."

We sat silently for a moment.

"If you could do anything in the world, what would you do?" she asked.

"Easy. I'd be a professional *kwarktaart* taster."

She laughed. "I'm serious."

I held her a little closer. "I don't know, Hannah. I really don't. I never did know; that's part of why I went into law. I enjoyed it well enough and was good at it. I mean, as good as anyone can be at memorizing things—which, for me, is pretty damn good. It made sense to me. I used to think it was my calling. Now I think it might be my curse."

"Well, imagine it. *Dreaming is free*," she said pointedly.

"I guess it's only fair you used my own line on me."

I thought about it for a little while, and she waited for me, content and patient.

"It's hard to think of anything outside of my degree. What am I even qualified for? I guess I could be a consultant or something, but I'm over the whole thing. I don't really want to practice law. I don't have any passions. How sad is that? I've been so busy trying to succeed, working toward my degree and then my advancement in my career, that I never even found any hobbies."

"What about before college?"

I shrugged. "I played basketball, but I wasn't any good, just tall. And I played video games, but I wasn't very good at that either. I like solving puzzles, solving problems, making things efficient." I shook my head, feeling hopeless. "I didn't think this would be my life. I didn't think I'd be in my thirties and so unhappy. I've failed in the most important way; I'm not happy. Well, I wasn't. Not until things changed. Not until I could see how to change them. And that's in part thanks to you."

She sat up and shifted to meet my eyes, her face sweet and soft and open and lovely, so lovely.

"I feel like I've been looking at life upside down for a decade. But now, I can see. I don't know what to do about it, not yet, but I can *see*. Do you understand?"

She nodded, her skin warm and rosy in my hand, her face tilted, eyes down.

"I'm sorry," she said quietly.

"Don't be. The realization is that much sweeter this way. I know now what I have to lose. I know what I have to gain. I know what I *want* even though I don't know how to get it yet."

"I believe you'll have everything you wish for, Charlie. All you have to do is reach out and take it."

I smiled and reached for *her* with the hopes of taking her. "Oh, is that all I have to do?"

She smiled back and leaned toward me, angling for a kiss. "That's all."

And so I took what she offered, starting with her lips.

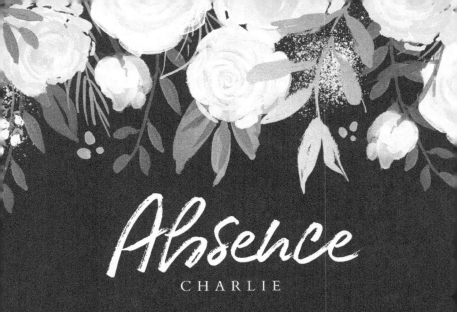

Absence

CHARLIE

The night was gone too soon, and morning came on its heels. The only real solace was that it was Sunday, and I'd be shirking work again.

Monday was going to suck for too many reasons to count.

Katie was off that day, leaving Hannah and me to fend for ourselves. And it was glorious.

Parenting with Hannah was fun.

It was so strange to realize that it *could* be fun. I'd never been a part of a unit that functioned like it did with her, and every minute with her had made me more and more confident that I *could* be a good dad, that I *did* know what to do, that I *could* have what I wanted.

I should have known things were going too well long before the knock on the door.

We were all in the entryway getting ready to walk to the Children's Museum when it happened, just an innocuous rap of knuckles on the front door. I answered with a smile that slipped off my face, turned down by the anchoring of my heart as it sank in my chest.

Mary's smile didn't falter, though it didn't reach her eyes. No, her eyes glinted with some secondary, alternative emotion more real than that false happiness on her face. Her dark hair was down and wavy, her clothes neat and unassuming.

Everything about her was a lie.

"Hi, Charlie."

I was stuck to the spot, staring at her for a long moment.

"Can I come in?" she asked, half-joking, the punch line—*to my own house*—left unspoken.

"No." It was almost a croak, my dry throat was sticky with shock and discomfort.

Her brow quirked. She still smiled. "What do you mean, *no*? I wanted to catch you when I knew you'd be at home, so we could … talk."

"No," I said, stronger this time. "Mary, you can't—"

"I can't what?" she shot, the truth in her heart surfacing, the brief niceties out of the way. "I can't see my children? I can't come into my own house?"

"For starters, yes."

"You can't do that! You can't dictate that. The keys to this house are in my fucking purse, and those children came out of *my* body. You can't tell me I can't!"

"Actually, I can. Your name's not on the mortgage, and you abandoned us. You forfeited your rights when you couldn't be bothered to show up for the custody hearing."

The color rose in her cheeks, but she schooled her face and tone. "Charlie, listen, I'm sorry. It's been … hard, confusing. I don't have an excuse; I realize that. But they're my kids, and I want to see them. This is my home, and I—"

"This stopped being your home the second you decided to fuck Jack," I said with a steely coldness that surprised her. "You don't get to show up here after all this time and change the rules—rules *you* dictated by your absence. That's not how this works."

"Mama?"

It was Maven, her voice small. I turned to look, my heart breaking, opening the door up without meaning to.

Hannah stood in the entry with Maven on her hip and Sammy peeking out from behind her. Hannah's eyes and face were full of emotion, tight and surprised and sad and protective as she and Mary stared each other down.

"Oh, look, it's the pretty nanny," Mary said with dry scorn that set the hairs on my neck on end, hackles up and tingling.

"Leave her alone," I growled.

She set her gaze back on me, heavy and assessing. "Ah, I see." She took a step back and shut her face down. "We're not going to get anywhere today, are we?"

"Not today. Not until you make an effort toward ending this once and for all. You can't pick and choose what you want to do, and I can't allow you to see them not without an arrangement through our lawyers."

Mary nodded once. "I want to be a part of their lives, Charlie. Seeing you at the hospital made me realize what I'd been missing. So, however you want to go about that, I'll do it."

My eyes narrowed.

It was too easy, and I wasn't buying any of it. She'd manipulated everyone she'd ever known, me worst of all, and I trusted nothing she had to say, even when it was the right thing to say.

Especially when it was the right thing to say.

"We'll see," I said.

"Yes, we will."

And she turned and walked down the stairs.

I closed the door with trembling hands, the solid thunk loud in the quiet entryway.

Hannah stood where she'd been, Maven resting in one arm, the other around Sammy's back, her face still just so *full*, as if there were a thousand things in her mind.

I couldn't blame her for a single one.

I raked a hand through my hair.

"Why was Mommy here?" Sammy asked quietly, subdued, from Hannah's side.

I knelt to his level and tried to find a way to explain. "I don't know, buddy. I'm going to try to sort it out with her, okay?"

"But she said she wanted to say hi. She said she wanted to see me and Maven."

The heat of the pain seared my lungs and heart until they ached and smoldered. "I know," I said, not much over a whisper. "I know, Sammy. And I want you to see her. We're going to try to figure out how, okay? Because since she left, there are some rules she has to follow, that's all."

He nodded and looked down at his shoes. "Okay, Daddy."

I cupped the back of his head and kissed the top of it, closing my eyes against the sting of it all, wishing there were an easy way out, wishing she hadn't come at all, wishing she'd just done the right thing and gone through the lawyers instead of coming here, hooking the whole lot of us and dragging us down into the depths with her.

But wishes and dreams, though free, couldn't be counted on.

I stood and met Hannah's eyes. "Hannah, I'm so sorry. I can't … I don't know why she …"

"You saw her? At the hospital?" she asked.

And I pinpointed the newest emotion on her face—betrayal.

I stepped into her and cupped her elbow. "I did. She was outside the door when I came back from getting coffee. I … I didn't want to worry you."

"You didn't want to worry me, or you didn't want me to know?" The question wasn't accusing; it was honest and hurt.

"I would have told you, I swear it." I searched her eyes, hoping she could read the truth in mine. "That night … Hannah, too much happened all at once. And the more I thought about it, the less important it felt. Nothing of consequence was said; all we did was argue. She wouldn't even come in to see Maven, not even when she was sick, and I … I …" My voice broke, and I swallowed the sadness, the disappointment, the urgent fear that I'd hurt Hannah.

But her worry slipped away, and she nodded once. "I understand. Just … please tell me what's going on. I don't want to be surprised, not by that. Not by her."

"Of course," I said and pulled her into a hug, sighing. "I'm sorry."

"So am I. Are you all right?"

I kissed her hair and pulled away. "Not really. But I will be."

"Yes, you will." And her smile made me believe it was true.

Busy Hands

CHARLIE

"Explain this to me one more time," I said, rubbing my eyes. My divorce lawyer and buddy from college, Pete, watched me from the other side of his desk. "From the top?"

"From the beginning."

He flipped through his notes and drew in a deep breath. "We filed your divorce papers—fault divorce under adultery claims—in June after she refused to answer your attempts to reach her. Two weeks later, we served her the papers at her workplace along with your settlement agreement, stating you would back-pay her for moneys paid into your home and agree to joint custody with you as the primary guardian. You were granted full temporary custody of the kids on"—he flipped the page—"August 12, and Mary didn't answer the divorce papers. We're still a few weeks from being able to file for a default ruling, but there's very little she could do to change things. She's relinquished her rights by not participating in the divorce or the hearing for temporary custody. I don't know many judges who would believe her if she came back around at this point."

"Do you think she knows? That we haven't filed for the default yet?"

Pete sat back in his chair. "It's hard to say. We haven't had any contact from her side at all. I don't even know if she has a lawyer. There's a possibility that she could file a petition to set the default ruling aside and have a judge her case, but the longer she goes on, the less likely it'll be that she can have it dismissed and actually start participating."

I sighed, the breath drawn from somewhere deep in my lungs. "I don't know what I'm supposed to do. She wants to see the kids, and I don't know how to tell them they can't see their mother. Don't get me wrong; I don't trust her, and I sure as hell think she should have come around a long time ago. But, if she's coming around now, I probably haven't seen the last of her. And if she's going to push for this, I don't know if I can say no with any just cause. I don't want to bar her from them out of spite, but I don't want to put them at risk either. I don't want her to weaponize them, but not allowing them to see their mother … it's cruel."

"Charlie, listen, you know how this works. If you set up a precedence, if you make any kind of agreement with her on custody now while everything is in flux, it could ruin everything. You can't give her an inch or she'll take it all. It's Mary we're talking about here."

"So keep her from them until the divorce is final?"

He nodded. "It's the only way you can guarantee control. If you want to let her see them after that, it's fair game."

"This is so fucked up," I said half to myself.

"I know. Welcome to divorce law."

"Thanks for your help with this. I know as much about divorce law as I do about cardio surgery." I tried to laugh, but it came out as a half-assed chuckle. "I don't know how you do it. M&A bleeds me dry on the regular, but it's nothing like trying to sort through people's failed marriages."

"Well, it helps when I work for the good guys. It's the times when I work for the assholes that I really have a crisis of conscience."

We both laughed at that, and I left Pete's office, so disgusted and downtrodden and lost in my thoughts that I wandered around Midtown a while, not wanting to go back to work.

Work was the last place I'd wanted to be for days. Weeks. Maybe ever.

I tried to fortify my will by reminding myself of the day I had gone in for the temporary custody hearing. The thought of seeing her for the first time since she'd left had left me sleepless for days, and the anxiety was so real, so pure, so horrible that I wondered if I'd break down in the middle of the courtroom. She was going to come, I'd been certain. She was going to fight, I'd known.

But she hadn't shown up at all, and that was somehow so much worse.

Now she wanted to see the kids after all this time, and I couldn't let her. I didn't even know if she truly wanted them or if she was just trying to manipulate me, but the image of their small faces when I'd barred them from their mother burned into my mind. It was no easier than the thought that she would hurt them, that she wasn't stable enough to be what they needed.

It just felt wrong, everything about it. Wrong and slimy and sinister.

And there was nothing I could do about it but wait it out.

HANNAH

Lysanne's mouth hung open like a fish as Charlotte's swing lost momentum.

I'd stopped talking for at least a full minute. "Say something."

She blinked, her gaping mouth turning into a smile. "I didn't think you actually had the nerve to kiss him, never mind ... all *that*."

I laughed and kept Maven's swing going evenly. "Honestly? That's all you have to say?"

"Of course not. It's like you don't know me at all." She shook her head and gave Charlotte's swing a heave. "I'm excited and nervous for you and Charlie. It's tricky, yeah?"

"It's only been a few days, so not yet. But I'm sure it will be. Though seeing his ex was probably a glimpse into the tricky."

"Sticky and messy. I can't believe she showed up like that. You said she hasn't seen them in months?"

"Since she left them all."

"Is she pretty?" Lysanne asked.

I nodded. "She's beautiful, dark hair and eyes, very ... I don't know the word. Cosmopolitan. Classy. A little scary. But what was strange was that I could *see* them together, but as if it were a different version of him, one I don't know."

"Like he had an evil twin?" she asked excitedly.

"Yes, a little," I said on a laugh. "They made sense, but they *didn't*. I don't know how to explain it other than that it was odd." My smile faded. "She's not fond of me; she made that quite clear. Not that I thought we might be friends. In fact, I hadn't even really considered her. She'd been gone for a long time ... so she was always ... *fictional*, just a piece of his past without a face. But she has a face now, a face and a presence, and I can already feel the weight of it between Charlie and me."

"I can see that. It's real now."

"He was with her all those years. These are his children with *her*. She is their mother. They're all facts I knew perfectly well, but I don't think I really understood them until yesterday."

Lysanne said nothing, her brows together as she pushed

Charlotte for a few seconds.

"I care for Charlie very much, and I've already accepted the truth of his past. It just shook me up to see her, to be confronted with her in that way."

"And that's understandable. How did Charlie take it?"

"Not well. He was far more upset than me, and the kids were too. Charlie has to shoulder so much." I shook my head. "It's why I didn't make a fuss when I found out he'd seen her at the hospital and didn't tell me."

Lysanne's eyes widened. "She was there?"

I nodded. "I didn't see her; she didn't want to see Maven."

"That's awful."

"I want to believe she has her reasons, but it's not easy to make excuses for her when I've spent so much time with the children, when I can see just how wonderful they are and how much they need her."

"Maybe her reason is just that she's a selfish bitch," Lysanne said matter-of-factly.

I laughed. "Wouldn't that be the easy answer? But nothing's that simple. Our hearts and minds are more complicated than that, with layers on layers of reasoning and feelings and motivation. There's always another side. There's always a reason, even if we can't agree on whether or not it's a *valid* reason."

"Well, I stand by my theory that she's just a terrible person—which, in my expert opinion, is *not* a valid reason."

I laughed again, and she smiled.

"I love you," I said, shaking my head.

"I love you too. What do you think will happen with Charlie? Long-term? I mean, you live there for the foreseeable future. What if things go bad? What if his ex comes around more? What if he does something like …" Worry touched her eyes, her brow, her voice. "What if he sleeps with her? What if he—"

I stopped her. "Lysanne." Discomfort snaked through me.

She clapped her mouth shut.

"We could worry about what-ifs all day and forever, and nothing good would come of it. I trust Charlie to tell me the truth, to be honest and open with me. It's all I really ask of him, all I require, and I believe he'll give that to me. In the end, if things don't work out, I'll go home. I don't want to take another job here, not after all I've been through."

"So you'll run away. It's the Hannah special."

I gave her a flat look.

"What? I'm only saying that this is how you like to problem-solve, that's all."

"I just don't want to trouble myself with worrying about things I can't control."

"I suppose that's fair," she conceded. "I'm proud of you for taking charge with Charlie though."

I sighed. "I was tired of waiting and not knowing and ... being uncertain. And, now ... I feel like I belong in a way. I haven't felt that in a long time."

She smiled. "I know. And I'm happy for you. What are you two doing tonight?"

"Oh, I don't know. He works so late, so much." The words were sadder than I meant to let on. "He took the whole weekend off, so I might not see him tonight. But that's probably good. We've been together for days, and a little time apart will do us good."

"You sound so pleased about it," she teased.

I laughed, but her face went pale as she looked past me.

"Is that ... oh my God, Hannah, look."

Quinton rounded the gate into the park, hands in his pockets, smile on his face, eyes on mine.

A surge of anxiety rushed through me, stopping my heart before it kick-started again, banging painfully against my ribs.

"Hannah," he called as he approached. "How about that? I was just on my way back from a late lunch with a coworker and thought I saw you."

It sounded rehearsed, pretend, like a lie.

"Hello," was all I could offer.

"Imagine that," he said, coming to a stop next to me. "Funny we keep running into each other."

"Yeah, funny," Lysanne said as she watched on, her jaw tight, still pushing Charlotte in the swing.

He briefly turned his gaze on her, hard and sharp, before looking back to me. "Can I speak to you for a second? Alone?"

Lysanne's eyes told me not to. Quinton's said he wouldn't relent. We were in public during the day. If ever there were a safe time, it was probably this. So, I nodded.

"Will you watch the children for me?" I asked Lysanne.

"Yes, of course," she answered, her words rigid.

And then I followed him to the hedges that lined the park.

He turned, smiling serpentine. "I want to believe it's fate that we've seen each other twice now."

I smiled politely. "Is there something you needed?"

Something flashed behind his eyes, something hot and forbidding. "Just for you to have coffee with me. I wanted to … explain. I mean, the least I can do is buy you a cup of coffee and offer you some understanding."

My smile faded. "I don't think that's a good idea."

His faded too. "Hannah, really, I only want to talk, I promise."

"There's nothing to discuss," I said with a sharpness I hadn't intended.

It set his shoulders and straightened his back, his chin rising just a touch. "I disagree. I think there's much to discuss. But I understand. Promise me you'll call if you change your mind."

I took a step away, my eyes narrowed and pulse rushing in my ears. "Goodbye, Quinton." I turned to walk over to Lysanne.

"See you around, Hannah," he said to my back.

I could feel the place where his eyes watched me. But by the time I was at Lysanne's side and summoned the courage to look, he was gone.

The weight of the moment left me in a breath that set my hands trembling as I lifted Maven out of the swing and held her close.

"What in God's name did he want?" Lysanne spat, picking up Charlotte as well.

We made our way to the sandbox—I had to sit down before I had no choice in the matter. "To take me to coffee."

"He … he what?" she sputtered. "What possible reason could he have for asking?"

"I don't know," I answered honestly, miserably. "Lysanne, I think I should tell Charlie."

Her mouth popped open. "You absolutely should not tell Charlie."

My brows knit together. "Why not?"

"Because he'll think you do *this* with all your bosses."

"Oh God," I breathed. "Surely he would believe me. Surely he trusts me."

"Hannah, his wife cheated on him. With his best friend. I'm sure he does trust you, but are you *certain* he'll understand?"

"I … I want to believe he will."

Lysanne's face was tight. She took a noisy breath through her nose and let it out. "Do you think Quinton will come around again?"

I considered it. "I didn't think I would see him at all, never mind twice. After what just happened, I think … I think maybe since I said no with some finality that it might be the end, but how can I be sure?"

"You can't, not with him." She watched me for a beat. "If it's not the end, if you see him again, *then* tell Charlie. There's no reason to upset the applecart for nothing, if it is nothing."

The idea relieved me—to avoid explaining something that I didn't want to speak of, didn't want to think of, something that had humiliated and scared me.

And so I said, "All right," hoping against hope that I was doing the right thing.

The rest of the afternoon was spent in the lighthearted, laughing company of Lysanne, and I found myself more thankful for her than ever. By the time we parted ways, I had all but forgotten about Quinton and the exchange and what Charlie might think of it.

I spent the evening with the children and dinner and baths and stories and bed. We were mostly alone—Katie had left before dinner to go home to her husband—and once the kids were asleep, the house was quiet. Big and empty.

Without any distractions, my thoughts wandered from Quinton—wondering over his intentions, over the truth of our *coincidental* meetings, over our past—to my future with Charlie.

And when I thought about Charlie, my thoughts led me to Mary, my worry keeping me from considering the good or the happy, only my fears and anxieties. I imagined her in this house, walking the stairs I found myself on, eating in the kitchen I walked into, drinking from the wine glass I sipped out of, sleeping in Charlie's bed upstairs. No, not Charlie's bed … *their* bed.

I'd never even been in his room; we were always in mine, every night. It was unspoken; neither of us wanted to share the bed upstairs and were perfectly content to stay in a space that was our own, untouched by memories of her.

I realized then, as I sat in Charlie's kitchen in my nightgown, that I'd only thought of his house as my home ever since I walked through the door. It had been so easy to never think of the house and the people in it in terms of the past, only in the present, as if it were all as new to them as it was to me. It had felt like *mine*, but it wasn't, and it never had been.

It was very likely that it never would be.

My stomach heaved at the thought—not at the possibility of not having it all for my own, but at the understanding that I'd been wishing for something without my consent or knowledge. I'd fallen into a dream in a way, and Mary's appearance had been a rude awakening.

I took a very deep breath and moved to the cupboard in search of flour and sugar and to the refrigerator for butter and milk and eggs, and I made my hands busy, made my mind think about something other than the truth of my circumstance, the truth of my heart.

Katie had kept the pantry stocked with supplies for me, always asking what I needed or wanted, sometimes anticipating what I was low on without my having to ask, and I was particularly grateful that night. Before long, I had puff dough in the refrigerator, cakes in the oven, and a dish of apples and raisins and cinnamon in front of me.

It was automatic and comforting, quieting my busy mind and uncertain heart with every stir, with the rolling pin in my floured hands, with the brushing of melted butter and sprinkling of sugar. It was a satisfying act of love and devotion, a remembrance of my childhood and family and home, a way to give a little piece of myself to someone else. And I lost myself in the motions.

I was icing the cakes when I heard Charlie's key in the door, and I couldn't stop my smile or the warmth in my chest or my feet from carrying me into the entryway with surprise and joy, my worries and fears gone the second I heard that sound that meant he was home.

His face mirrored my heart.

We almost rushed each other, and in a breath, I was in his arms, the chill of the night clinging to his coat and lips and hands. But I kissed it away as best I could.

Charlie leaned back to look over my face. "Hello to you, too."

I chuckled and kissed him again, swiftly and sweetly. "You're home early."

He shrugged. "Yeah, I hit my limit. I thought having a few days off might freshen me up for work, but I'm afraid it did the opposite. It's literally the last place I want to be." He held me closer. "Wanna know the first?"

I tilted my head and pretended to think. "Hmm, the subway?"

He shook his head. "Guess again."

"The bath?"

That one he considered. "If you're in it, then one hundred percent yes." He kissed me again.

I breathed him in, feeling like I hadn't seen him in days, not just a few hours, and he seemed to do the same, his hands and lips telling me he'd missed me, that he wanted to be there just as much as I wanted him there.

The kiss ended with a sigh.

Charlie ran the strap of my apron through his fingers. "What are you baking?"

"I'm icing *oranjekoek*, and I have *appelflappen* in the oven."

"I have no idea what you just said, but it smells amazing."

I laughed. "Orange cake, apple … how do you say …" I made my hand open and shut like a book. "Flip. Ah … pocket?"

"Like a turnover?"

"Yes!"

He smacked his lips. "I want to eat all of that. Lead the way."

I threaded my fingers into his and pulled him into the kitchen. "How was your day?"

"Awful. I don't even want to talk about it. How was yours?"

"Good. I saw Lysanne today, which is always nice. I feel … full after spending time with her. Do you know what I mean?"

"I think I do." He pressed a kiss into my hair when we came to a stop.

I smiled up at him as he looked over the cake, layered with almond paste and topped with pink glaze.

"So this is ... let me guess ... the orange cake?"

"Yes, that's right. I don't know why it's called orange cake though; it's pink."

"Does it taste like oranges?"

"A bit. It has candied orange peels in it, but the word *oranje* is a color. The fruit is *sinaasappel*," I added with a shrug.

"So ... an orange is an apple?"

I laughed. "The first we ever saw of oranges, they came from China, so the word they made for it was Chinese apple."

He shook his head and sat at the island. "That is so weird."

"I know." The timer went off, and I turned for the oven. "*Zo gek als een deur.*" I pulled out the *appelflappen* and set the pan on the stove. "As crazy as a door."

Charlie laughed from deep in his belly. "Because everyone knows doors are irrational."

"My *oma* has so many funny sayings. Like, when we were little, if a joke was made we didn't understand but we laughed, she'd say, *Jij bent lachend als een boer met kiespijn.* You're laughing like a farmer with a toothache." I demonstrated, holding my jaw like my tooth hurt and laughing awkwardly.

That earned another laugh.

"The best was when we asked about her health, and she'd tell us she was *kiplekker*, which translates to *chicken delicious*. But it just means healthy."

"*Lekker* everything."

"*Lekker* everything is right."

I put an *appelflap* on a small plate, and he took it with hungry eyes. "My mouth is actually watering."

I watched his tongue wet his lips as he picked up the pastry. When he took a bite, he moaned, eyes closing.

"God, how do you do that?" he asked around a bite.

I laughed, pleased by his pleasure. "Years of practice, three or four generations of recipes, and a lot of butter."

He ate with enthusiasm, and I picked one up to join him.

"Should I get used to you being home this early?" I asked before taking a bite.

Charlie shrugged. "You shouldn't, but I might be past the point where I care about getting in trouble for ditching. For a minute at least. I'm still riding out Maven's hospital visit. How awful is that? I just think I've hit some sort of limit, some kind of wall. I don't know how to go in there and pretend anymore."

My heart squeezed as it sank. "I'm a distraction."

His brows drew together. "No, you're saving me."

I shook my head, setting down the pastry, no longer hungry. "No, Charlie. I'm … I don't want to be the reason you fail. I don't want to hurt you."

He was off his stool and walking toward me before I could move, his eyes dark and burning, his big hands on my face, tipping it up. "Hannah, you might be one of the best things to have ever happened to me."

My sinking heart rose again, though it still ached.

"Do you understand that I've been *stuck*? I've been stuck in my life and in my head for longer than I think I even realized, but you've shown me how much more there is, how many things I've missed while my head's been down. You opened a door I hadn't realized was closed, and now that I've seen what's on the other side, I can't go back. I can't pretend I don't know. I knew I wanted a change, but I didn't realize just how badly I wanted more from life until I caught a glimpse of what *more* is. My kids, my family, happiness. That's what I want. So please, don't say that. Don't say you're bad for me, not when you've shown me everything *good*."

I didn't know what to say, my throat tight and eyes searching his.

But I didn't need to speak. Because when he kissed me, it banished every thought from my mind.

CHARLIE

I kissed Hannah and told her without words that I needed her. I held her face and spoke through my fingertips, telling her she had changed me just by existing. And as she kissed me back, I knew she understood.

All day, I'd been thinking of her. Every tick of the clock had been noted in my mind as I counted down the seconds until I'd see her again.

I'd been consumed. I had far less control over my heart than I had known.

I didn't even want it back. I'd gladly relinquished it to her.

Hannah would never hurt me. She would never betray me. It was a truth, innate and instinctive, the knowledge that she only wanted my happiness and I only wanted hers. And I would never go back again. I would never be manipulated again, would never be used, now that I knew what more there could be.

The kiss went on, deeper and deeper. She leaned into me, breathing heavy and loud, hands roaming down my chest, around my waist, up my back and down again, never pausing. Mine weren't still either, my fingers thirsty for her skin from earlobe to breastbone and to places I couldn't reach, not with her clothes in my way.

So I rid her of them.

Her apron was first—the one thing I was loathe to remove, reminding myself to have her wear this once with nothing else. My fingers twisted around the tie at her waist and tugged to loosen it, and I pulled it over her head. She wore a nightgown the color of a storm cloud, thin and gauzy, the fabric hanging on the peaks of her tight nipples, the curve of her warm breast soft and supple in my palm. My free hand found her bare thigh, fingertips slipping under the hem and to the swell of her ass.

And her body bent to me, giving and giving and giving, never taking. Just letting me take, letting me touch, letting me slip my fingers into her panties to touch the hot center of her, to trace the slick line and the silky bud, to slip inside her warmth, a prelude, a promise of more, a promise I would fulfill the moment my cock was free.

She moaned into my mouth, the softest, sweetest of tremors of her breath and tongue and lips against mine, and I held her against me, pressed the confined length of me to her, moaning right back.

I stepped with her to the island, and once her weight was against it, she brought her leg up and spread it, opening up, letting me in, my thumb on her clit and my fingers deep inside her until her hips rocked and breath sped and I couldn't take it anymore.

I let her go, breaking the kiss to push her panties down her legs, the two of us panting, her hands on my chest and pupils dilated. My hands were a blur as they unfastened my belt and pants, my lips finding hers; they couldn't stay away, couldn't leave her alone, couldn't stop. And then the length of me was free, one hand gripping my base, the other pushing her nightgown up her long thighs, her legs spreading again and hips angling for me. She was on the tips of her toes, and I bent my knees, looking for the connection, feeling for the heat of her, sucking in a breath through my nose when I found it, hot and wet and waiting.

I flexed and filled her up.

Her ass was propped crudely on the counter, but she didn't care, just wrapped her legs around my waist and whispered my name, begging me. But she didn't have to beg. I'd give her anything, everything.

With a roll of my hips, I pulled out and slipped in again, her shaking hands fumbling with the buttons of my shirt, desperate to touch me. But I didn't stop, didn't stop moving, didn't stop pumping, couldn't have stopped, not with her hips immobilized, pinned like they were. She was at my mercy, and I would give her what she wanted, what she needed. I flexed again, grinding when I couldn't get any deeper, giving her the pressure she sought. My hand wanted skin as much as hers, sliding under her nightgown and to her breast, to her nipple.

She gasped, breaking the kiss, and I leaned back to watch her, the vision burning in my mind—the arch of Hannah's long body, her chin up and eyes closed, neck curved, nightgown hanging on my wrist as I touched her, the creamy white skin of her stomach, the place where our bodies met, the sight of the length of me disappearing into her.

It was too much to control, too strong to contain, my hips moving faster as her brows pinched and she whispered her pleasure. She tightened around me once. I thrust harder, jolting her. She tightened around me again. I moaned her name. And she burst around me, pulsing and flexing and drawing me into her until I came with a rush, my nerves firing, eyes slamming shut as I drove into her with such force, she cried out in the sweetest gasp of ecstasy I'd ever heard.

I leaned into her, wrapping my arms around her to bury my face in her neck, my breath ragged and body still pulsing inside her. Her arms wound around my neck, fingers in my hair, breath against my skin, sending goosebumps over me. And I breathed her in, the smell of comfort and sweetness, and I knew with absolute certainty that there was never anywhere in the world I'd been so happy than in her arms.

"I missed you," I whispered into her hair.

She kissed my neck with smiling lips. "It was only a few hours."

"I know, but I missed you anyway."

"I missed you too," she whispered back. "Take me to bed, Charlie."

I leaned back and gazed into her sleepy, sated face. "What about the kitchen? All your hard work?"

"I don't care. I don't care about anything but you."

All I could do was kiss her, kiss her with an aching heart and blissful joy, and do anything she asked of me.

Refuge

CHARLIE

The next morning, I kissed Hannah goodbye at my doorstep and practically skipped to work. If it'd been raining, I'd have done a sad imitation of Dean Martin and gotten soaked while I tap-danced and spun around light posts with a lovesick smile plastered on my face.

I was affected. With every day, I was changed.

I'd spent the whole night with Hannah in my arms, and the second the front door had closed behind me that morning, the only thing I could think about was getting home to her again. In my mind, I knew I was infatuated with her. Years and years of being miserable had left me with a surplus of emotion and desire, it would seem. Logically, I realized that a large part of how I felt was chemical.

But deep down in my heart, it was more. I knew that too. This wasn't just an overlooking of flaws or an easy connection with someone who meant nothing.

She meant everything to me.

It was blind devotion I felt, and all because I trusted her.

For the first time in my adult life, I had found someone to trust implicitly and completely. In the time I'd known Hannah, I'd come to call her my friend. I'd let her in and learned from her. I had turned that corner as I chased my happiness, and this time, I saw her just ahead of me. And I wanted to reach for her hand. I wanted to pull her to a stop. I wanted to finally hold happiness in my hands after they'd been empty for so long.

It was crazy to feel so much. I knew it. I recognized it. But after so long with someone who had hurt me for sport, my heart was willing and ready to be treated with respect and care.

It was like stepping into the sun for the first time.

I gave myself a pass on the rush of emotions when I considered that, this far into Mary's and my relationship, we had nearly been engaged. But where my feelings for Mary had been thin and superficial, I felt Hannah in my marrow. I needed her to fill up my heart every night, like cracked earth dried to dust, soaking up every drop of water to try to find itself whole again.

The workday was slow even though I was busy with my mounting workload. I'd been fielding questions about said workload and my absence too, conversations with people whose eyes were shrewd and probing. Because no one could possibly understand.

"Sick kid," I'd say. "You know how it is."

I wanted *the life*, and I couldn't get it without shirking my job, so shirk my job I would, and I wouldn't have a single regret about it.

Maven was fine, though I'd keep making excuses to get home to my kids every night, to tuck them in and play trucks and Barbies and to sing songs while they bathed. I wanted to be home on the weekends for lazy Sundays and outings and walks and laughter and *time*.

That was really what I wanted and needed most of all—time.

And I had precious little to spare.

So I sat at my desk, wishing I were home, wondering what Hannah was doing while the kids were at school, wondering what we would all do when I made it home, considering how early I could actually leave without getting me in any more trouble than I was already in. I wanted to avoid dealing with that for as long as possible. The clock was ticking on me; I could feel it.

It was early afternoon when I looked up from my desk like I'd felt *her* coming.

Mary's head was high as she walked through the office toward me, every face in the room turned to her. I was almost too shocked to believe it was actually her, to believe I hadn't manifested the vision of her as some sort of penance for my happiness.

But she was real, very real.

My heart dropped into my stomach, and my stomach hit my shoes.

I stood before she reached me, rushing toward her as anger surged in my chest, grabbing her by the elbow to wheel her around.

"God, Charlie, what the hell?" she hissed. As if she had any right to be upset.

I tossed her into a conference room—the office was completely silent and watching—and shut the door behind me.

"What in the fuck are you doing here, Mary?" I threw her elbow back at her.

Her face bent and flushed in anger. "I came to talk to you where we could be alone."

I pinched the bridge of my nose, trying to find some level of composure. "You could have called. You could have emailed. We could have set up a fucking time, but you *cannot* just show up at the house and my job. *This has to stop.*"

She had the nerve to look hurt. "I'm sorry. I just didn't think you'd answer me."

She wasn't entirely wrong.

"What do you want?" I asked.

"To talk."

I glared at her and swept my hand, as if to say, *Be my guest.*

Mary took a deep breath and softened her face. "I know what I did was wrong. I've made a lot of mistakes, and I don't know how I'll ever make it up to you and the kids, but I want to. So what do I have to do?"

"Right now, it's not really an option. Not until the divorce is final."

Something flashed behind her eyes, but I couldn't place what it was before it was gone again.

"I couldn't sign those papers, Charlie. You ... you were always the steady one, the one who knew what to do and what you wanted. You always did the right thing. But I only ever felt ... *stuck*. Do you know what I mean?"

I nodded once, not knowing if I was standing in a trap or an apology.

"I just ... I don't know if I want a divorce."

"Well, you don't really have a choice. It's filed and done." I bit my tongue. The last thing I needed was to give her any information she didn't have about what could happen if she changed her mind and tried to fuck things up even worse.

She looked wounded again. "I thought ... Charlie, you were always there, even when things were bad."

"And you thought I'd just wait?" I laughed, a dry, joyless sound. "How many years would you have gone on fucking Jack? Because my guess would be *all of them*, as long as you could get away with it. And I'd be willing to bet that if he hadn't cut you off, you and I wouldn't be standing here right now."

Tears glistened in her eyes. "I'm sorry. I really am."

She stepped toward me, but I held my ground, jaw clenched.

"I just wish there were some way to change your mind." Her eyes were big and sad, her face turned up to mine, her hand reaching for my fingers as she closed the space between us.

I jerked my hand away from hers and took a step back, staring down at her with a raging fire burning in my chest.

And in an instant, the doe-eyed woman was gone, her face twisting. "I can't even believe this, Charlie. You're doing this? You're doing this to me—refusing me? You really want to throw me away?"

"*Are you fucking kidding me?*" I screamed. "Mary, for fuck's sake, *you walked away! You left us! You* threw *us* away. And, now ... now that it's almost finally, *mercifully* over, you want to come back and try to make amends? Try to manipulate me again into doing what you want? You're out of your fucking mind."

"This is about that nanny, isn't it?" she asked with flaming cheeks and a quavering voice.

And then it was all too clear. "I don't know, Mary. Is it?"

"You're fucking her, aren't you?"

"That's none of your goddamn business."

She fumed. "Those are *my* kids, Charlie. *Mine.* That is *my* life she's living."

"That was never your life. You never wanted to be a mother. If you hadn't gotten pregnant, we wouldn't have gotten married. If it hadn't been an accident, you wouldn't have ever had kids. And *you* were the one who wanted Maven. I'm not sorry for that, I could never be sorry for that, but that was *your* plan, and for what?"

"*Because I was losing you!*" she howled, angry tears streaming down her cheeks. "You pulled away, and I thought you would leave me! But I knew, if we had another baby, you'd stay. I knew you'd stay, and you did."

My hands and face tingled from the surge of adrenaline that shot through me. "And the second you had Maven, you started fucking Jack," I said coolly. "So much for happy endings."

She drew herself up, her breath shuddering and eyes flinty. "You can't keep me away from my children. I'll go to therapy with you, have a mediator, whatever you want. I'll do whatever you want. Maybe once you're through with that cow-faced girl who's standing in for me, you and I can see if we can start again. You're my family. *Mine*. Not hers."

I took a breath. I let it out. I pulled myself together and said, "Have your lawyer talk to Pete."

Mary stood there before me for a long, angry moment until I opened the door and stepped aside, staring her down. Only then did she leave.

My hands quaked as I walked back to my desk with a face of stone, refusing to make eye contact with anyone. It was only when I was sitting at my desk that I let out a troubled sigh.

I dropped my face into my hands, plagued by anger and guilt and madness and confusion.

This was what she did. She did her best to make everyone feel like it—whatever *it* was—was *your* fault, not hers. I thought it was because she actually believed it herself. She believed she wanted to see the kids, maybe even believed she still held some claim on me.

The reality was that when she left me, she had given me an out from a situation I never should have gotten myself into in the first place. There was nothing to mend, nothing to repair, nothing left in my heart for her but resentment.

But there was one thing I couldn't deny, no matter how much I hated her.

They were her children, too.

If she wanted to see them—even if her motivation was impure—she should be able to. Not for her sake, but for the kids. She was their mother, for God's sake, and they needed her. What kind of father would I be if I didn't let them see her?

The thing was that she couldn't really see them, not yet, not without some sort of a plan. I just hoped to God she'd reach out to Pete so we could get something together.

Confusion and loss washed over me, followed by a wave of guilt.

I wanted to tell Hannah. I wanted to go home that very minute and lose myself in her. I wanted to confess everything, tell her all that was in my heart, all that Mary had said, all the ways she'd hurt me and used me and betrayed me.

But I couldn't. I couldn't because I was afraid.

I had happiness in my grasp, and now that I'd found it, I had everything to lose. I trusted her with my heart, but how could I trust her with my past? How could I expect her to bear the weight of my divorce and my ex? My baggage would have her packing hers and leaving me.

If I lost Hannah because of Mary's interference, I would never, ever get over it. If Mary found a way to hurt me through Hannah, I would never, ever be able to let that failure go.

I'd promised Hannah I'd tell her everything, and I decided then that I would. When the time was right, I would tell her everything. But for right now, I would hang on to what I had with all that I had.

"Charlie, we've got the Logan Tower conference call in five," one of my colleagues said as he walked by.

I sat and nodded, trying to gather myself as I gathered my paperwork for the meeting, swearing to myself that the minute I could get out of this building, I would. And I'd go somewhere I was safe.

To Hannah.

HANNAH

I kissed Sammy's forehead and answered three more questions before he let me leave, and the second I turned around from his door, I saw Charlie.

He stood at the foot of the stairs looking up, his face bent with pain and hurt and worry, and I felt mine match.

"Charlie, what's—"

But he was already taking the stairs two at a time, his eyes on mine like a tether until he pulled me into his arms and kissed me with desperation, holding me against him, breathing heavy, lips hard against mine.

And I let him, let him take what he needed, kissed him back with as much fire as he gave until he broke away and pressed his forehead to mine.

"Charlie," I breathed.

"I need you," he whispered and crushed my lips with his.

So I gave myself to him.

He swept me into his bedroom and into his bed, the room he'd shared with *her*, and with every kiss, he banished her. With every breath, he filled his lungs with me. And I knew the room was no longer theirs any more than his heart was.

Our clothes were shed with no care until we were skin-to-skin. His hands were rough and fast, spreading my legs, gripping his length to press it against me. And with a hard flex of his hips, he filled me to the hilt, not pausing to savor the feeling before rocking his body.

"Hannah," he said, voice as rough as his hands.

"I'm here," I breathed as he slammed into me, sending a shock up my body, my breasts jostling from the force.

His frantic hand held my face, fingers in my hair, body urgent and speeding toward his edge, his face so full of despair and desolation and emotion that I sped toward mine. And when I felt him throb inside me, when he bowed his head and came, I was right behind him, riding the wave of his body until the surge faded.

He collapsed on top of me, his weight pressing me into the bed, his face buried in my neck and heart thundering through his rib cage. And for a long time, I held him. I let him be, let him feel, let him just exist there in my arms with no questions. None I spoke at least. My mind was full of them, circling and whirling and whispering doubt.

He rolled us over, separating us with the motion, pulling me into his chest where he held me, kissed my hair, slipped his thigh between mine to wind our legs together.

"Are you all right?" I finally said quietly, the most innocuous thing I could say.

"Better now," he answered.

I pressed a kiss to his chest.

"Bad day, that's all. I just wanted to be here where things are simple."

My heart ached, and I leaned back to look at his face. "I'm sorry things are so hard. I only want you to be happy."

His brows tightened. "When I'm here, I'm happy, and when I'm not here, I'm not happy. And the only thing that's changed is you."

He was afraid, I realized; he thought I might go, that I might leave.

He didn't know just how impossible that would be.

So I touched his face, wishing I could wipe his worry away with my fingertips. "I'm here, Charlie. I'm not going anywhere," I whispered.

He pulled me into him for a kiss, a kiss that told me he didn't believe me. So I kissed him back and told him without words that he should.

The Other Side
HANNAH

A few days passed, as did Charlie's desperation. He would come home from work by eight or nine every night, sometimes even early enough to read the kids stories and put them in bed. He was cavalier and irreverent with his time—gone were the days of Charlie's long hours and absence—and I couldn't stop wondering what price he would pay.

He hadn't told me what had upset him that day, hadn't done anything but spend every spare moment with the children and with me. That was something I couldn't complain about at all.

The weather had gotten cooler, the leaves almost completely fallen as November drew to a close. My mind was on Charlie while I walked to get the kids from school with a smile on my face as I daydreamed about the moment when he walked through the door. I imagined the smile I'd come to know so well, and my own smile just stretched wider.

I greeted Caitlyn, who stood behind the counter at the preschool with a look of surprise on her face.

"Hey, Hannah. Can I help you?"

My brows drew together. "I'm just here to get the kids."

Her eyes widened. "What do you mean? They're not here."

Cold fear slid through me, trailing goosebumps across my skin, seizing my heart. "I'm sorry?"

"They ... they're not here. Their mother picked them up two hours ago."

The chill was replaced with a rush of fire. "Oh God," I breathed.

"I didn't think ... I mean, she's on the list. I thought it was strange—she's only been in a few times *ever*—but I didn't have instructions or ..."

I didn't hear the rest of what she said, not with my mind racing, not with my shaking hands reaching into my bag for my phone.

Caitlyn was still talking, apologizing.

I reached for her hand on the counter and squeezed it. "It's all right. I need to call Charlie, okay?"

She nodded, but I barely saw her. My eyes were on my phone, my feet flying and breath huffing as I rushed out the door and down the sidewalk.

Charlie picked up in just a few rings. "Hey," he said happily, his voice warm and velvety. "I was just thinking about you."

"Mary has the children," I said, the words tight.

A pause from Charlie. "She ... what?"

"I just went to pick up the kids and they weren't there. Charlie, she has them. I don't know what to do. What should I do?" Panic rose in my chest, climbing my throat.

"Go to the house right now. I'm on my way." His voice was calm, succinct, direct—a lawyer's voice—though underneath that was an undercurrent of the panic he couldn't so easily hide.

"All right," I said softly.

"Hannah, it's going to be okay. I'll be right there."

The words soothed me, the certainty, the comfort he offered. "Okay."

We hung up, and I almost ran, my calves and shins burning from exertion and restraint, my heart pounding with fear and worry.

It took me three tries to unlock the door, the key unsteady in my hand, but when I got it open and stepped inside, I found myself completely unprepared for what I found.

In the hurried walk home, I had imagined scenario after horrifying scenario. But never had I imagined Mary would be sitting with Maven and Sammy in the kitchen, eating ice cream.

I froze in the threshold of the kitchen, my eyes wide and staring at the scene without understanding what I was seeing. Their faces turned to me—two with smiles, one without.

Sammy dashed out of his chair and over to me, cheeks high and ice cream on his face. "Hannah! Mommy came back, and she took us to the park and then got us *ice cream*! She got me *ah-sash-io*— it's green, like a turtle—and Maven got strawberry 'cause that's her favorite. Come here! Come say hi!" He took my hand and pulled me into the room.

Mary's face was all sharp angles, her voice with just as much of an edge. "Oh, look. The pretty nanny. Hope I didn't alarm you by picking up *my* children a little early."

"She really *is* pretty, isn't she, Mommy?" Sammy beamed.

"Yes. Very pretty." Mary stood, squaring her shoulders.

"What are you doing here?" I asked.

Her eyes narrowed. "In *my* house, you mean? With *my* kids?"

"Charlie said—"

"I don't really care what Charlie said. These are my children, and he can't stop me from seeing them."

Sammy clung to my hand, his smile gone. "Hannah?" he asked,

unsure, a little afraid.

I bent to his level and smiled at him. "Why don't you go get the iPad and put on a show? Daddy will be home any minute. That way me and your mommy can talk, yeah?"

He nodded, glancing back at his mother before turning to leave.

When I stood, Mary looked murderous—lips flat, cheeks flushed, brows knit together and eyes flashing. "So sweet, aren't you? No wonder Charlie's fucking you."

I sucked in a stinging breath, my neck and face hot. "He'll be home soon, and you can talk to him. This is none of my business, and I'm none of your concern."

She laughed, a cheerless, empty sound. "From where I'm standing, it looks like you're in my seat, *Hannah*." She said my name as if it were bitter poison.

"That seat was empty when I got here."

"You bitch—" she started.

The door opened and closed with a slam. "Hannah?" Charlie called anxiously.

"In here," I said, not breaking eye contact with Mary.

His footsteps grew louder, stopping completely right behind me. "What the fuck are *you* doing here?" he growled, the sound so deep and angry, it took everything I had not to turn around.

"Just had an afternoon with my kids that's all," she said, as if it were that simple.

"You're out of your fucking mind, Mary," he shot.

"I told you at your office the other day that I wanted to see them."

Cold awareness climbed my ribs. Now I knew why Charlie had been so upset. He'd seen her, and he hadn't told me. He hadn't told me when he'd promised me he would.

"You can't just—"

"I *can*!" she shouted. "I can, and I will. *You* can't tell me I can't see my children because I will find a way."

"Are you threatening me?"

He stepped around me, and I chanced a look. His face was hard as stone.

She stepped toward him, everything about her screaming, but her voice was still. "You know me better than that, Charlie."

"You never did take no for an answer. Guess I shouldn't be surprised, but somehow, I always think you'll be better than you are."

"Oh, don't play high and mighty with me, you arrogant prick. You're the one fucking the help."

"That's *enough*!" he roared, stepping into her, arching over her. "Kidnapping the kids isn't going to get you what you want, don't you realize that? If you would play by the fucking rules, you could have anything you want. But if you won't, you're going to end up with *nothing*. I'll make sure of it. Do you understand me?"

Her face bent in furious desperation. "I can't have what I want, Charlie! I can't! It's all gone, so I'll take what I want. I'll take it back from you, from *her*," she spat the word in my direction.

"No, you won't." He grabbed her by the arm and steered her away, their arguing unintelligible as they headed for the door.

I stayed put, my hands icy and heart thundering. Their fight reached me in waves from the foyer as the volume grew and lessened, and when Maven reached for me, I picked her up, taking her to the sink to clean her up.

The door opened and slammed closed, and Charlie was in the room a few seconds later, rushing to me.

Maven was on my hip, the two of us in the circle of Charlie's arms, his hand cupping the back of Maven's head, his lips pressing a kiss to her hair, then my forehead.

"I'm sorry," he whispered. "I'm so sorry."

"Why didn't you tell me?" I asked.

He knew what I'd asked without any explanation. "I'm so sorry," he said again, his voice miserable and pained. "Hannah ... I ..."

"Don't you trust me?"

He looked into my eyes, his truth plain and clear. "I do. But Hannah, I've never ... I don't know what I'm doing." The words were tight as he fumbled with what to say and how to say it. "I'm afraid. That's the bottom line. I am scared that I'll do all of this wrong, take a wrong step, and I'll lose you."

"You'll lose me if you keep things from me."

He nodded, his eyes down. "It's too much to expect that you would put up with all of this for me, not when you could have so much more with someone else. Things could be easier. I ... I don't know that things will ever be easy with me, Hannah. Not with Mary. Not now that she's come back after all this time just to drag us both through hell."

I shook my head, my heart aching. "I care about you, that's why I'll *put up with this*. But you kept this from me when I'd asked you not to. I'd told you I didn't want to be surprised again, not by her. Not because of something you could have avoided just by trusting me."

"I know," he said miserably. "I know. I'm so sorry."

"So am I."

We were quiet for a moment, Maven curled up between us, the silence heavy with our thoughts.

I backed away and passed Maven over. "I'm going to go check on Sammy."

His face was pained and sorrowful. "Are we ... are we all right?"

"I don't know," I answered as honestly as I could. "Let's talk later, okay?"

"Okay."

I kissed him on the cheek and left the room, looking for Sammy, lost in my thoughts. I found him in his bed and climbed in with him, not really listening to his cartoon.

The last hour replayed in my mind, the swing of emotions—from fear to relief to anger to hurt—leaving me feeling exhausted and confused. Because even though I was upset with Charlie, I understood why he hadn't told me. It was no excuse—he *should* have told me—but if I'd been in his shoes, I would have grappled with the decision too.

Not to mention, I had my own secrets.

But Mary *was* a lot to handle. I wondered how he'd dealt with her for so many years, though I imagined when she got her way, she was more compliant than she'd been of late. Now she felt threatened—that much was perfectly clear—and she was making a stand, showing Charlie she would throw anything she could at him, and me too. I was just another tool for her to use to hurt him.

Because that was also perfectly clear. She wanted to hurt him. She didn't love him whether she said she did or not. She only wanted the thing she couldn't have, the thing she felt entitled to, regardless of what choices she'd made.

Charlie left me alone with my thoughts the rest of the afternoon.

I took Sammy downstairs, finding Charlie in the living room with Maven in his lap, reading her a book. Sammy joined them, and Charlie passed me a small smile. I returned it but didn't stay.

I headed into the kitchen. Katie was there, her face lined with worry. She'd come home from grocery shopping just after Mary left, finding Charlie and the story of what Mary had done. She had questions—many, many questions—and I answered them all as I gathered up ingredients and began to mix them together. Sugar and flour and eggs and water and questions and answers and conflict and confusion—all were poured together and folded and combined and kneaded until they were unrecognizable from their beginnings.

During dinner, Charlie filled the air with questions for Sammy, who answered them with exuberance. It was an effort on Charlie's part to let me be, and I appreciated that allowance more than he could know.

He put the kids to bed that night, but before he went upstairs, he stopped at the sink where I stood washing dishes and asked me with his words and his eyes if we could talk when he returned.

I waited for him in the living room, sitting on the couch with my eyes on the dark fireplace, not sure how I felt or what I wanted or how we'd gotten here. It was such a simple request—to tell me the truth. It was all that I'd asked and the one thing he hadn't given me.

Charlie came in a little while later and sat next to me, facing the fireplace, our eyes forward and the room silent.

He didn't speak for a minute. Neither did I.

"I should have told you," he finally said.

"Yes, you should have."

He took a deep breath. "She came to work the other day. Why, I'm not sure. Just to … I don't know. Press me to give her what she wants. She thought … she thought when she came to the house on Sunday that I'd let her in, that I'd give her whatever she asked for. And when I said no, it triggered all this. Her coming to the firm, her taking the kids, her showing up here."

I didn't say anything.

Charlie kept talking. "She tried to tell me she didn't want a divorce, that she wanted to make it all up to me. Said she wanted to make it up to the kids. And that's the hard part, Hannah. As much as I don't want to see her, as much as I would love to cut her out of my life forever, I can't. They're her children. She's not going anywhere, no matter how badly I want her to. Technically, I'm still married to her. And that fact is why I didn't bring it up. I'm not afraid of her. I'm afraid of losing you. I have nothing to hide, no secrets to keep, but I'm scared that it will all be too much."

"You'll lose me if you lie. You'll lose me if you shut me out."

"I know," he said quietly. "Hannah, it will not happen again. I promise you that."

"You promised me that once before."

He nodded. "But now I understand what I'm promising."

My eyes were forward, but I reached for his hand. "She won't leave you alone. None of you."

"No, she won't." His thumb shifted against mine. "I don't know what to do about her. I have custody of the kids, and that won't change, especially not after her behavior—from her leaving us and staying gone for so long to her taking the kids without telling me. I emailed Pete, my lawyer, and told him what happened. I can bar her from picking up the kids, but I can't stop her from showing up here. I can't stop her from confronting you, and that makes me feel so sick and angry and helpless."

"Don't worry about me. I can deal with her if I have you to stand behind me."

"I'm here, Hannah," he said gently.

I turned to meet his eyes. "Even when it's hard? Even when you worry about how I'll react?"

He nodded. "I just want to protect you from all this."

"But I don't need protection. I need you to trust that I'm here, that I'm not going anywhere."

"I know. And I do."

I touched his cheek, felt his worry. "You don't have to be afraid."

"I wasn't—until I had something to lose." He turned his face to kiss my palm. "You make me feel safe. You make me feel right, like I can be what you see in me. And I don't want to go back. I don't want to go back to that place, back to that life. I just want you."

My heart beat against my ribs like it was reaching for him. "I'm here, and I'm yours."

And he kissed me with thanks and longing that I hoped would keep him from closing me out again. Because I could forgive a great many things, but if he didn't trust me, we would be lost before we truly had a chance to begin.

Say the Word

CHARLIE

I sat at my desk the next afternoon, feeling like a stranger, feeling split. There were two versions of me—before Hannah and after Hannah—and the version whose chair I sat in had become so foreign to me, I didn't even recognize him anymore.

The other version of me, the version I wanted to be, was focused only on the kids, on Hannah. The afternoon before replayed in my mind over and over—from the moment I'd heard the paralyzing fear in Hannah's voice to the moment I'd slipped into sleep with her arms around me and her heart wounded, my children safe in their beds.

But questions plagued me, worry occupying every thought. Would Mary show up again? Would she leave us alone? Would it ever be over? Were the kids safe? Was Hannah safe?

I'd removed Mary's name from the daycare list with the help of my custody ruling, and I'd called to have the locks changed, which helped my peace of mind. Just not enough. Not enough to allow me to pretend I was all right with leaving them.

Hannah had said they'd be safe at school with Mary's name off the list. And she'd assured me that she and I were fine, that we'd be all right.

I wanted to believe both things were true, but I didn't, and there was nothing anyone could say to convince me.

Everything felt *wrong*, as if I'd taken a turn onto a street I didn't recognize.

As I sat there with my imagination running away from me in the last place I wanted to be in the entire world, I couldn't find a way to believe it was all right. I couldn't find a way to stop the chugging anxiety, the circle of thoughts. My eyes stared through my computer, the alerts from my emails unnoticed as they dinged and animated the top of the screen. My phone rang, but I barely heard it. Someone walked by, calling me in for a meeting. I didn't look up.

Everything *was* wrong, I realized. And I had to fix it.

There was only one way, and decision and action rose in my chest.

What I wanted was at my fingertips, and I could have it.

All I had to do was reach out and grab it.

The old version of myself didn't even put up a fight, just stepped aside. Because I knew what I wanted, and I knew how to get it.

I wanted to be home with my family. I wanted to protect them. I wanted to give them my time and my love. And I couldn't do any of that from the cubicle where I sat with my phone ringing endlessly on my desk.

I gathered my things, assessing my finances in my head. I wrote an email to my boss and resigned. I stood and pulled on my coat, ignoring my colleagues as they passed by my desk, staring. I never picked up my phone.

Instead, I walked out of the room, out of the building, away from my old life and into my new one.

With every step, I felt the weight slip off my shoulders. With every block, I thought of Hannah and the life I wanted, the life I wished for. As I ran down the subway steps, my smile stretched so wide, my cheeks hurt.

Because I was going to do what my heart wanted. And there was only one person who I wanted to tell. I wanted to tell the girl who had changed my whole life from the second she walked through the door and showed me what love could be.

I wanted to tell Hannah, and I wanted to ask her to stay with me. Not as my au pair and not for the kids.

For me.

HANNAH

Katie and I parted ways at the sidewalk outside the house with a kiss on the cheek and a promise to see each other after the Thanksgiving holiday weekend. The days were growing shorter, the sun slipping away earlier and earlier, painting the sky in fiery colors that matched the leaves left on the trees.

I kept myself busy rather than think too much over everything between me and Charlie or Charlie and Mary, instead spending the day preparing for Thanksgiving, which was the next day. Katie would be off; the kids out of school; Charlie away from work. And we had a long weekend ahead of us with food and togetherness. And I was looking forward to it, hoping we could begin to mend the fissures between us.

But the silly, foolish girl in me hadn't quite gone; she'd just been hiding. And the moment I felt hope was the moment I was reminded that hope was a trap.

Mary was leaning against the brick wall outside of the school, watching me with her hands in her jacket pockets and her ankles crossed in front of her. The sight of her sent adrenaline racing through me and my heart knocking against my ribs in warning.

But I held my chin up, setting my jaw. "Hello, Mary," I said flatly as I approached and stopped in front of her.

She watched me for a moment.

"I can't quite imagine that you have nothing to say, so go ahead and say it."

Her eyes narrowed. "They wouldn't let me pick up the kids."

"It's not my doing."

"No, it's not. *You* don't have any rights," she said, as if I didn't know.

"He doesn't want to keep you from them. You must know that."

She shrugged, not meaning it. "He told me he'd keep me from them unless I worked with his lawyer. He also told me to stay away from you. I almost believed he actually cares about you."

I stood a little taller against the jab but didn't speak.

"I hope you enjoy playing house with my family. You can be the pretend mommy to my kids and the make-believe wifey to Charlie. But they'll never be yours, not really."

"I don't know that they'll ever be yours either. At least one of us knows it."

Her lips flattened. "Live it up while it lasts, pretty little nanny. Because it won't last long."

I held her eyes for a drawn-out second. "Anything else?"

She pushed off the wall. "I'll see you around. Same time, same place?"

Everything about her was tight and hurt, wounded and angry, and I realized it then, understood the flint in her eyes and forgave her for it. I didn't like her—I never would; we would never be friends—but I forgave her.

"I'm sorry you're unhappy," I said quietly, sincerely.

Mary froze, her eyes hard as diamonds. "You don't get to feel sorry for me. You have no idea who I am or what I've been through."

"It doesn't matter. I just hope you find a way through it."

"Well, aren't you just a fucking angel?" she shot, though her voice shook just a little. "How does the world look from up there on your high horse?"

I shook my head. "Mary, I don't want to hurt you. None of us wants to hurt you."

"Too fucking late," she said as she blew past me and away.

It wasn't until she was gone and I'd made my way inside that the initial shock wore off, leaving me with the fear and anxiety that seemed to always follow encounters with Mary. She'd come for the children again and waited for me, waited just to hurt me, told me without completely saying so that she'd do it again.

She wanted to hurt me because hurting me would hurt Charlie. She wanted to hurt me because she saw me as a threat. She wanted to hurt me because she was hurt.

I was shaken, gathering the children and signing them out, talking to Sammy as if nothing were wrong, as if it were a normal day. I thought Maven might know different. She asked me to hold her, and when I picked her up, she wrapped her little arms around my neck and hung on to me, the comfort and warmth of her so overwhelming, it took everything I had to stave off my tears.

I was so lost in emotion that I didn't hear my name, not at first. The second time *he* said it, a chill worked down my spine.

I turned to the sound, finding Quinton trotting across the street toward me.

The blood rushed from my face; I knew because it tingled, prickling cold splotches across my skin.

He was tall, dark, gorgeous. Dangerous with that razor-sharp smile.

"Hey, Hannah," he said when he reached me, stopping close to me, too close.

I took a step back, trying to move around him. "I'm sorry. I'm in a hurry," I said, shaken and desperate to leave, to get home where it was safe.

But he moved to block me. "Come on, Hannah. You don't even have a minute?"

"No, I don't." I tried to step around him again, but he wouldn't let me. "What do you want?" I asked, my voice trembling.

He reached for my arm. "I think you know. I've missed you."

I jerked away, but he didn't let me go. Sammy squeezed my hand. "Please, leave me alone. Let me take the children home."

"I'll walk with you."

I glared at him, fighting back tears. "My answer hasn't changed, and it won't. I'm with someone."

His dark eyes rolled with thunder. "The blond? Your boss?"

My panic rose with the bile in my throat. He'd seen us. He'd followed me.

"Hannah?" Sammy asked, his voice small and afraid.

I looked down at him, squeezed his hand. "It's all right. We're just going."

But when I tried to pull away from Quinton again, he wrenched me into his chest.

"Tell me," he said through his teeth. "Is it him?"

"Yes," I answered with more strength than I felt.

Everything about him hardened—his eyes, his jaw, his lips, his fingers digging into my arm. "So, you cock-tease all your bosses, is that it?"

"Do you harass all of your au pairs?" I shot.

"No, only you."

I twisted away, but he grabbed my other arm like a vise, holding me still.

"Let me go."

"I wonder what the agency would think about you and your new boss."

"Go ahead and tell them," I spat. "Just leave me alone."

And I was so overwhelmed, so wholly focused on my escape, that I never saw *him* coming.

CHARLIE

I didn't think—there was no time.

The second I saw the way *he* had ahold of her, when I caught a glimpse of that tall bastard with his hands on her, with my kids between them, I snapped, panic and fear and anger boiling up in me like a furnace.

I bolted toward them, reaching them before either registered my approach. But when he did, his face flashed in surprise, and he loosened his grip enough for Hannah to rip one arm away.

I wedged myself between them, looking down at him with so much rage, I thought I might combust.

"Get your goddamn hands off her." I bit out the words, my nerves firing and fists squeezed tight.

The minute he let her go, I shoved him away from her with enough force to send him wheeling back a few steps.

When he found his footing, he straightened up, smoothing the front of his suit coat.

"Who the fuck are you?" I asked, shielding Hannah and the kids with my body.

He smiled, a smug, cruel expression. "Hannah didn't tell you about me? Before she was with you, she was with *me*."

Fury flared hot and desperate, betrayal crackling at the wavering edge. "Hannah, take the kids and leave."

"Charlie—"

My eyes were on his. *"Hannah,"* I warned, and I felt her step back. "Now, what the fuck do you want?"

He watched her; she hadn't left. I could feel fear radiating off her and knew she wouldn't go without me.

"Just wanted to see our girl here," the asshole said when he finally looked at me. "Things haven't been the same without her. She does that to a man. Know what I mean?"

My stomach heaved, my lungs emptying like I'd been hit.

"I didn't, Charlie. I never—" she stammered from behind me.

"You know," he kept going, his voice hard and body squared, "Hannah and I bump into each other all the time. I can't believe she didn't tell you about me."

Realization washed over me, pulling me under.

And he saw it in my face, his smile widening as he goaded me. "She's too pretty, too sweet, too *innocent* for me to let her go without a fight. She's irresistible, just like her cakes and cookies. I know I couldn't help myself; it's no wonder you couldn't either."

Two steps, and I had him by the shirt. "Shut the fuck up," I hissed, the words wavering.

But he laughed. "Sorry, *Charlie*. You're not the first. I doubt you'll be the last."

With a roar, I cocked my fist and let it fly, connecting with his jaw with a crunch of my fingers and a smack of skin.

He reeled back, hand shooting to his face. The burning in my hand traveled all the way up to my elbow, every bone in my fingers screaming.

"You stay the fuck away from her," I shot, punctuating the command with a jab of my finger.

He held his jaw and spit a gob of blood on the ground.

"Why are you doing this?" she cried at him from behind me.

His eyes moved to her and changed, darkened, pinned her down.

"I'm not accustomed to being told no."

I took a step toward him. "Well, get used to it. Now get the fuck out of here."

He stood for a long moment, sizing me up as I fumed, chest heaving, nostrils flaring, my blazing hand begging through the pain to hit him again. And he must have seen it.

He rolled his shoulders to adjust his coat, as if it were a board meeting rather than an assault on the street. And with a last look at Hannah—a look that sent an icy chill up my back and to my hackles—he turned and walked away.

I waited until he was across the street and half a block away before I found the will to turn around. The heat of my anger had burned down, leaving nothing but cold ashes.

Hannah was crying, and so were the kids.

I bent to Sammy and pulled him into my arms. "You okay, bud?"

He nodded. I stood, holding him into my side, reaching for Maven. I didn't touch Hannah.

"Are you all right?" I asked flatly. "Did he hurt you?"

She shook her head, her eyes down and guilty.

"You lied to me."

"Charlie, nothing happened."

"Have you seen him? Since you left?"

She nodded. "Twice. He seemed harmless. I swore I would tell you if I saw him again."

I took a long breath, my face tight, chest tight. "You've shut me out for not telling you about Mary, and now I find out about *this*? You weren't home when I came home from work early, so I thought you might be getting the kids. And that was what I found."

He was touching you. He'd touched you before.

I knew the look on his face because I'd worn it. I knew desire for her because I'd felt it.

I raged on. "Not only did you keep the truth of why you'd left your last job from me, but you also kept the fact that he was *stalking* you to yourself. I don't know if you trust me any more than you believe I trust you."

Pain lit her face. "Charlie, I—"

"Did you sleep with him?"

She jerked back like I'd slapped her, her face paling. "I can't believe you would ask me that."

"That's not an answer," I snapped. "Is this some sort of game to you? Am I a pattern? A conquest? What?"

"Of course not," she blustered. "I didn't sleep with him."

I looked into her eyes and I wanted to believe her. Deep down, I might have. But in that moment, I could only think of how familiar it all felt. I'd been here before, and it was a place I never wanted to be again, a place I never thought I would be in with Hannah.

Yet here I was.

"Please, tell me you believe me," she begged, her eyes shining with fresh tears.

"What am I supposed to think, Hannah?"

"You're supposed to trust me."

"Like you were supposed to trust me?" I volleyed, my lungs burning and aching. "It's no wonder you didn't tell me."

The blood climbed up her pale neck and to her cheeks. "Like you didn't tell me about all the times your *wife* came to see you?"

"That's different. I wanted to *protect* you from her."

"So you say, but you wouldn't be the first married man who wanted more from me. How am I to know you haven't been seeing her? She came to the school again today, did you know? She waited for me, humiliated me. She wants *you*, and she thinks I have you, but now, I'm not so sure."

It was my turn to be shocked. "I can't believe you'd say that. I can't believe you'd think I could want anything to do with her after what you've seen, after what she's done."

Tears spilled down her cheeks, her voice broken. "I can't believe you don't believe me when all I've ever done is try to make you happy. She hurt you, and I never would. And you know it. *You know it.* I've done nothing but be accepting of your circumstance, but at the first sign of trouble, you accuse me of the worst, jump to conclusions—"

"I'm not jumping to anything. He *said*—" I tried to say over her, but she didn't stop.

"It's not fair, Charlie. I asked you to trust me, and you can't. Not with Mary, not with this. You'll believe whatever you want, and maybe it's just because she broke you beyond what I can mend. But I won't defend myself against this. Not this." She took a shuddering breath. "Do you trust me or don't you? Do you believe I've slept with someone else, that my feelings for you are anything but what I've said, what I've shown you?"

And in my hurt and rage and confusion, I said the last thing I should have. "I don't know."

Her chin trembled, brows bent from the weight of her sadness as she drew in a breath. "Then, that's all there is to say."

"I guess so," I said coolly and turned my back on her, my children in hand, leaving her standing on the sidewalk behind me, watching me walk away.

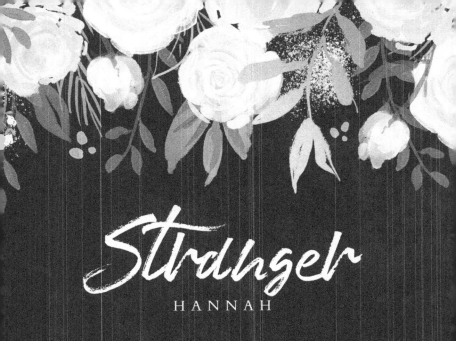

Stranger

HANNAH

I watched Charlie walk away through a sheet of tears, my heart split and spilling.

He'd cut me open. The pain and shame of what Quinton had done wasn't enough; Charlie had had to accuse me of the very thing I'd tried so hard to escape.

I couldn't follow him. I couldn't go home because home wasn't home anymore.

So I turned on feet that didn't feel like my own, unable to find the will to stop myself from crying, my face streaked with heavy, fast tears, sobs caught in my throat.

I didn't stop until I was at Lysanne's door. I wasn't embarrassed when her employer answered the door and ushered me in. I wasn't relieved when Lysanne rushed into the room and took me into her arms. Because there was nothing to be done, no way to go back.

She took me into her room and sat me on her bed, coaxing the story out of me. And once I started speaking, I couldn't stop, not until it was over, the words pouring out of me like my tears.

All the while, I pictured Charlie's face, the hard glint in his eyes and the set of his jaw. The betrayal and anger, his disappointment and disgust. After being hurt by Mary and then Quinton, I never thought he would hurt me too.

And that cut had been the deepest of all, the one that had emptied the reserve of my will, the pain so deep, I could barely breathe. I pressed my palms to my chest as if I could stop the bleeding, but it was no use.

Lysanne pulled me into her, smoothed my hair, whispered, *Shh*, offering me no words of comfort because there were none.

And so I cried until I was empty, until my breath evened and my temples ached.

"What will you do?" she asked quietly as she rocked me.

"I … I don't know. I have nothing with me, none of my things. I … I can't go over there." My panic rose again, filling the empty space in my chest. "I can't. I can't see him right now. How am I supposed to see him? I can't … I can't—" I choked on a sob.

"Shh, it's all right. You don't have to see him. I'll go get your things, okay?"

I took a shuddering breath and nodded.

"And what will you do after?"

I pulled away and looked down at the tissue in my hands. "I want to go home."

She sighed, her hand on my back and her face sad. "I thought you might."

"I never should have come here. I never should have left home. Because I don't belong here, and I never did, no matter how I felt for a moment that I might. I just … I can't believe …"

"I know," she offered. And I knew she did. "I think … I think maybe you should file for a restraining order against Quinton."

"It doesn't matter. I'm leaving."

"Maybe it doesn't matter for you, but what about the next girl?"

I met her eyes, pleading, "Please, I can't talk about this right now."

She swallowed, nodded, bowed her head. "I'm so sorry, Hannah."

But I couldn't speak. Because I was sorry too, sorry for things I could never change, sorry for things I'd lost, knowing I would never get them back.

CHARLIE

Two hours passed.

Hannah didn't come home.

I didn't want her to.

The betrayal ran deep, too deep to measure, the pain of being lied to—especially about this—overwhelming and final.

It was a cardinal sin, the ultimate breach of faith and trust. And I couldn't see her. Not yet.

Calm resolve wound itself through me, a resoluteness I knew wouldn't be relieved without some amount of time, if ever. And I had no idea how we would face each other or what either of us would say.

I wasn't ready to find out.

I'd come home with the kids and turned on the television, sitting with them on the couch—Sammy tucked into my side and Maven in my lap. The fact that my children had been present for all of that was salt in the wound. They were both shaken and subdued. Sammy was silent and still, which in itself was a testament to how he'd been affected.

I stared through the television, my mind turned inward and my nerves shot. She felt like a stranger to me, and I was a stranger to myself.

When the doorbell rang, we all jumped.

Hannah, was my first thought. My second was that it couldn't be her—she had a key—followed by a conflicting wave of relief and disappointment.

I left the kids in the living room, not expecting who I found when I opened the door.

It was a girl, a tall girl with long chestnut hair and impatient, accusing hazel eyes.

"I'm here for Hannah's things," she said curtly with a Dutch accent.

My heart stopped. "Lysanne?"

She nodded once, her eyes cutting through me.

I stepped out of the way to let her in, and she rushed past, heading for the stairs.

"Let me show you down," I offered.

"I'll manage," she shot.

I followed her anyway. "Is she … is she all right?"

Lysanne wheeled around, her face full of wrath and fury. "I'll not speak of her. Will you please leave me to do this alone?"

I took a step back, straightening up. "Of course."

"Thank you," she spat and hurried down the stairs.

I watched her go and ran a hand over my mouth.

It was then that I realized it was probably over. If you'd told me yesterday that I wouldn't be completely beside myself at the prospect of losing her, I would have said you were insane. But now, after she'd lied to me, after *that man* had said what he said, I found myself too full of doubt to fight the feeling.

So I walked back into the living room and sat with my children until I heard Lysanne struggling up the stairs with Hannah's suitcases.

I made my way over to help, but she shot me a look that would have been enough without her telling me that she had it.

And as she wheeled them toward the door, I found myself asking the one thing I needed to know.

"Is she coming back?"

Lysanne turned to pin me with her hazel eyes and said, "No, Charlie, she's not."

And then she was gone, and so was my future.

Gone, Baby, Gone.

HANNAH

"I hate this," Lysanne said sadly from where she sat on her bed, watching me pack the few things I'd unpacked the day before.

"So do I," I answered simply, honestly. "I think we can both agree that this isn't the career path I was meant to take. It's time I go home and put all of this behind me."

Lysanne shook her head. "But what will you do at home?"

"For a while, maybe nothing. I need to sort through what happened. And then maybe I can figure out what I want, what I want to do, who I want to be. Being here was supposed to help, but it's only made things harder, and now … now I'm more lost than ever." Tears burned the corners of my eyes and the tip of my nose. "This has been too hard, too much, and I don't want it anymore. I never should have come here."

She slipped off the bed and to my side, taking one of my hands in both of hers. "Don't say that," she said gently.

"But it's true. Nothing good has come of this, only pain."

"Charlie wasn't all pain, was he?"

"No, but that's why losing him is so much worse. It would have been easier if he'd been like Quinton. It would be easier if I could hate him. But I don't hate him at all." I tried to take a breath, but it hung and skipped in my chest. "Even after he hurt me, I can't hate him. I think because … because …" I looked down at my hands.

"Because you love him."

I nodded, the tears I'd wanted to keep away filling my eyes. "And he's not wrong. I should have told him just as much as he should have told me about Mary. I asked him for honesty I couldn't give to him and demanded trust I couldn't return."

She frowned. "You not telling him about Quinton isn't the same as him keeping Mary from you."

"But it is, in its way. This is why he doesn't trust people. She hurt him that badly, betrayed his trust in the most unforgiving way. And as far as he believes, I did something too close for his comfort."

"You're making excuses for him."

"No, I'm not," I insisted. "I haven't forgiven him for what he said and did. I only mean that I understand him. But there's nothing left to say. I'm ready to go home—I was ready before I met Charlie. I don't belong here, Lysanne. All I have left for me here is you, because I've lost Charlie. What am I supposed to do? We hurt each other too badly to go back." I shook my head. "I'm through fighting. It's time to be done with it."

"But what if he was sorry? What if he tried to make it all right again? What if he told you he didn't mean what he said?"

"How could I believe him? He told me the truth. He didn't know if he could trust me. He lied to me about Mary, kept his meetings with her from me. He accused me of seducing him and Quinton, took *Quinton's* word over my own. That's what hurts the worst, and, now … now, I'm just tired. We're a dead end, Charlie and me."

"I just … I wish things were different."

"So do I. But Charlie looked into his heart and couldn't see the truth. I know he's been hurt, but I never did anything but give him everything he'd asked for. And all I asked for was this one simple thing—trust that I'd proven to him I was worthy of—and he couldn't give it to me." Hot tears spilled down my cheeks, and I swiped at them, hating them, hating the gaping hole in my chest and my aching heart that sat inside.

"I don't want you to go," she said with tears of her own in her eyes.

"I know. But it's time. You're all that's left for me here, but unless we get married, I'm afraid I can't stay in America."

She laughed at the joke, though her face was still weighted, her eyes shining. "Well, I suppose the good news is that you'll be home in time for *Sinterklaas*. There could be worse times to go home. You'll be busy enough to avoid thinking about the whole mess."

"Yes, and I'll be glad for the distraction."

"I'm going to miss you."

I pulled her into a hug. "I'll miss you too. I'll send you some things, yeah?"

She sniffled. "Make me some stroopwafels. Real ones. And chocolate letters. And little people cookies."

"Is that all?"

"How about I send you a list?"

I laughed and pulled away. "All right."

"I love you, Hannah. And I'm so sorry."

"I love you too," I said and pressed my forehead to hers.

An hour later, we said goodbye on the stoop, our tears fueled by the truth that we didn't know when we would see each other again, spurred by our sadness and guilt and sense of failure. Nothing had gone as planned, and as I watched rain streak the window of the taxi, I wondered how things had gone so far off track.

The truth was that I didn't want to leave at all. I wanted to tell the taxi driver to turn around and take me to Charlie. I wanted to tell him everything—how I felt, the truth about Quinton—and beg him to take me back. But I couldn't. I couldn't force him to trust me, and I shouldn't have to.

So I would go home and pretend that none of this had ever happened, however impossible that would be. Because I had changed, and he was the reason. He was the reason for everything.

But he'd never been mine, not really. We'd only been playing house, just like Mary had said.

I'd just realized it a little too late.

CHARLIE

Music played quietly in the kitchen late that afternoon as I ate Thanksgiving with my children. We were otherwise alone.

Completely alone.

Hannah was gone, leaving a silent void where she'd been, and I was so aware of that fact, like a phantom limb. My brain couldn't find a way to connect with the truth—she wasn't there, and she wasn't coming back.

I'd spent the evening before with my children, but once they had fallen asleep, I'd dragged my numb body down the stairs, the house quiet as a tomb.

A glass of scotch hadn't been enough. Three had had me feeling like maybe I would be all right. Four had found me sitting at the foot of her bed in front of her dark fireplace, staring at the soot and ashes, wondering how I'd lost her, how I'd lost my faith and hope, losing my happiness along with it.

I'd woken the next morning in her bed, reaching for her. But her side of the bed had been cold, and I was alone.

I'd thought loneliness was bad after Mary. But until Hannah, I hadn't felt truly loved. And the difference made my isolation infinitely harder to endure.

As I sat with my children over Thanksgiving, I found I had so many more regrets than things to be thankful for.

Sammy had a thousand questions I couldn't answer. Maven even asked a few, which were almost harder. She said so little, and the sadness in her eyes was almost too much to bear. I knew that feeling.

Their hearts had been broken, too.

Katie had left instructions and prepped food in the fridge, so I'd busied myself that afternoon managing it, hoping maybe it would cheer us all up to have such a familiar, comforting meal. But it hadn't. I saw Hannah everywhere—in the apple pie with a braided lattice, in the cookies she'd made, in the empty chair where she would have been sitting, in the bouquet of pink roses that had already begun to wilt, their petals opening up and curling at the ends. And she wouldn't be there to replace them.

I was alone, and I'd lost the one thing besides my children that meant anything.

And I'd never forgive either of us for it.

That night, I ended up in her room again, though this time, I built a fire, sat in her bed that smelled of her, of home.

I'd been hurt before in what felt like another life, and those old wounds hadn't healed. I'd thought they had. I'd thought Hannah had healed me. But at the first sign of trouble, they'd split open again, raw and angry and unforgiving.

And I couldn't find a way to stitch them up again.

Home is Here

HANNAH

The flight had been long, but I hadn't gotten much rest, not with my thoughts on Charlie, on the children, on my regrets as I ran away, ran home.

The realization that had hit me hardest of all as I flew over the Atlantic was that I truly loved him. I loved him even though he'd hurt me. I loved him even though he wasn't free to love me back. I loved him for how he loved his children and how he'd made me feel. I loved him for wanting me, for giving me a glimpse into a life where I belonged to someone and where they belonged to me even if I couldn't keep them.

And what hurt the most was that it didn't matter that I loved him because I'd had no choice but to leave.

I waited for my bags at the carousel with bleary eyes, rolled them outside in the drizzling rain, took a train home, my mind on Charlie all the while, on all the things I'd left behind in New York, on all the things I'd left in Holland that I would come back to.

Once I was out of the station, I climbed into a waiting taxi, and when we pulled away, the driver made small talk, asking after my trip, if I was home for the holiday, about my family, and I didn't want to speak of any of it, didn't want to talk, especially not about America or what had happened there. But I smiled and answered all the same.

It was good practice for when I got home.

When I unlocked the door, and called, *"Hallo,"* I found that my entire family was home.

They flooded into the entry, smiling and shining and tall and blond, and with every kiss and hug and word of Dutch rather than English, I found my spirits lifted, my heart filled back up for the moment.

Everyone was talking at once—Mama shushing my eight-year-old twin brothers, who were bouncing, asking what I'd brought them. Annelise, my older sister, and Johanna, my younger sister, talked and laughed, watching me with eagerness to get me alone and hear the real story. Oma hugged me and told me I looked hungry—she always smelled of vanilla and cinnamon and home. And Papa wrapped his arm around my shoulders, whispering that he'd missed me.

Mama ushered us back to the kitchen, our favorite room of the house.

We all sat at the long table in the dining room that Mama and Annelise had set with cookies and pastries and tea and coffee. They flitted around, gathering extra spoons and napkins and generally fussing about.

"Did you see the Statue of Liberty?" Bas asked.

"Did you eat a hot dog from a cart?" Coen asked before I could answer.

"Did you get mugged?" Bas asked just after.

Papa tsked. "Boys, maybe give Hannah a little breathing room."

They made faces at him.

"If your mouth needs something to do, eat a cookie."

They didn't need to be told twice. It became an instant sport to see who could eat the most at once.

Johanna beamed at me from across the table. "I can't believe you're home!" *I can't wait to hear why,* her face said.

"I've missed you too," I said with a laugh.

Annelise and Mama finally sat, beaming down the table at me.

"How's the shop?" I asked. "Who's keeping it today? I didn't think you'd all be home."

Mama laughed. "As if we would stay at work when we knew you would be here. We've all missed you terribly, Hannah."

I smiled back. "I've missed you too."

"Sara and Julia are at the shop. They said to tell you hello. We'll see them tomorrow, I think."

"What had you rushing home without warning?" Oma asked without malice or accusation. It was just her direct, nosy, caring way.

Everyone was silent, and a flush crept up my cheeks.

"I was just homesick, Oma. It would have been my first holiday away from home."

"Bah," she said with a wave of her hand. "You're not a baby, Hannah, and I know you better than to think you would turn tail and run home because you missed your mama. Did something happen? You're all right, aren't you?"

"Yes, Oma, I'm all right," I said a little too quietly.

She didn't believe me, and her face told me so.

But as she opened her mouth to argue, Mama cut in. "Hannah, how is Lysanne? How was America? We got your postcards, but I want to hear about the adventures you had."

Oma gave Mama a look. "But I want to know—"

"Have a cookie, Mama," Mama said pointedly.

Oma took the cookie Mama thrust at her, dipping it into her

coffee with a look on her face.

I smiled at Mama gratefully and launched into stories about New York and Lysanne, skirting around my failed jobs and the tangled up mess that had ended it all and sent me home. By the time I was finished, Oma looked fit to burst with questions, and I pushed away from the table.

"If it's all right, I think I'd like to shower and lie down for a little bit."

"Yes, of course," Mama said, seeming relieved. She'd seen Oma, too.

Papa took my bags upstairs, and Mama hooked her arm in mine, taking me up behind him.

"Are you all right?" she asked quietly when we were out of earshot of the rest of the family, still chatting noisily in the kitchen.

I leaned into her. "No, but I suppose I will be."

She nodded. "I'm here, if you want to talk. I'm always here."

"I know," I said, wishing I could tell her everything, deciding that I would once I had it all sorted out myself. "I'm sorry to come home so suddenly."

"Why ever would you be sorry? I never wanted you to leave in the first place," she said on a laugh. "New York is too far away. I missed you, my angel. And to have you home now is the best gift I could get. I can't even explain how I was dreading the holiday without you. It wasn't going to be much of a celebration with one of my children missing." She squeezed my arm, pulling me a little closer.

"I missed you too. I shouldn't have gone away, Mama," I said, tears springing from out of nowhere as we came to a stop outside of my room.

She searched my face. "Don't cry. And don't regret going. I don't believe that things happen for a reason. The idea of fate never appealed to me; I wish to be the master of my future. But everything that happens to you, good or bad, is a chance to learn and grow. So don't wish to change the past. Just consider the future and use what you've learned to make yourself stronger. That's all you can do. That, and wait for time to pass so that whatever hurt you has time to heal."

She didn't wait for me to answer, just pulled me into a hug, and I sank into her arms, closing my eyes, fighting my tears back for just a few more minutes until I was alone.

Mama let me go just as Papa came out of my room, pressing a kiss into my hair before taking Mama's hand and leaving me alone with my thoughts.

My room was as I'd left it—a comfort and a curse. Because even though it was the same, I had changed. I'd never be the girl who had last sat on this bed and daydreamed about her future with blissful, dreamy romanticism.

I didn't unpack—I was too tired, too worn—just set my suitcases on their sides and opened them up, digging through them for my toiletries and a change of clothes. Down the hall I went and into the shower, turning the water as hot as I could stand it, waiting until the stream ran lukewarm before dragging myself back out.

I dressed sleepily in leggings, an oversize sweater, and tall, comfortable socks, braiding my damp hair. And by the time I made it back to my room, I found both of my sisters sitting on my bed, cross-legged and excited.

Annelise motioned to the door. "Close that, and tell us everything."

I sighed. "Lise, I'm so tired. Can we talk later?"

"No. Now, close the door! You know Oma is listening."

Johanna laughed. "She can't stand not knowing."

I sighed again, this time even heavier. And then I closed the door because the looks on their faces said they wouldn't be leaving until I told them.

"Move over," I directed as I approached, climbing into bed with them.

"What in the world happened?" Johanna asked. "You really are all right, aren't you?"

I only had a small smile to offer as reassurance. "I'll be okay, but right now … no, I'm not all right. Not really."

"Start at the beginning," Annelise ordered and leaned in to listen.

And so I told them. I told them about Quinton and his advances and my leaving. I told them about Charlie, about who he was and how I cared for him, about Mary and the kids and the whole ordeal, all the way to our fight and my trip home.

I left out the part where I loved him.

They watched me, hanging on every word, every twist and turn, only offering gasps and gaping mouths and the occasional noise of disdain, especially whenever I brought up Mary.

"You haven't spoken to him since you left?" Annelise asked.

I shook my head.

"You care for him very much, don't you?" Annelise watched me with eyes that saw too much.

"Yes, very much."

"Have you thought about calling him?" Johanna asked.

"A hundred times, but I won't. I can't, not after the way things ended. There's nothing for either of us to say." I took a breath. "I never should have taken the job, not after Quinton. I knew it the second I first saw Charlie, but I thought I knew better. And in the end, I hurt him, and he hurt me. It was a dangerous situation, and I didn't even think twice, just jumped in. I shouldn't have left home in the first place. Everything that happened in America was a mess, and now I just want to forget all about it."

Tears dropped off my lids, too heavy and fast for anything but a free fall from my lashes.

Johanna reached for my hand. "I'm sorry, Hannah. I'm sorry this happened."

"Mama said not to be sorry. She said I should be glad it happened, but it hurts too badly to be ready for that."

"Well," Annelise started, "Mama's very wise about such things."

"Yes, she is."

She nodded and moved to climb off my bed. "Come on, Johanna. Let's leave her alone to rest, yeah?"

"Yes, of course," Johanna answered, hugging me tight before she followed Annelise to the door.

Annelise smiled from the doorway. "You sleep. We're going to make you *oliebollen*, so they'll be ready when you wake, and we'll be sure there's enough that you can eat them until you're sick—with some leftover."

I chuckled. "That actually sounds perfect."

And then they ducked out of my room, leaving me alone.

I slipped under the blankets and listened to the sound of rain pattering against my window, wishing for things I could never have.

Wants & Needs

CHARLIE

The next three days were a hazy drift.

Katie was off through the weekend, and I was on my own. I threw myself into caring for Maven and Sammy. Having full hands helped—the moment they woke, I would be busy and grateful. Grateful for their love and for the way they filled my aching, bruised heart. For the purpose they gave me.

But the moment they were in bed and the house was quiet, I would find myself lost again, counting my mistakes and regrets. And, when the morning came and the sun spilled through the crack between the curtains in a wedge, I would wake and wish for Hannah.

But there was nothing left to be done.

Monday morning, I woke with the sun, lying in my bed for a long while, staring across my pillow to the empty one. It used to belong to someone. It used to be warm every night, but now it was cold and empty. It used to belong to Mary, but now … now it belonged to a girl, *the* girl, the one who had left, the one I'd sent away. The one who had hurt me.

I slipped out of bed and padded downstairs to make coffee, my hands moving without any direction. And once the machine sputtered out a cup, I sat down at the kitchen table, my eyes fixed on the dying roses in the window.

I hadn't had the courage to throw them out.

The front door opened, and Katie walked in with a smile that faded when she saw me in the kitchen.

"Hey, Charlie," she said with false levity, setting grocery bags on the kitchen island. "Everything okay?"

"No, Katie, it's not."

"What happened?" she asked as she approached, her face tight with worry.

A sigh escaped me that explained everything. She took a seat next to me.

"Hannah's gone."

"What? Charlie, what in the world?"

I nodded and drew in a tired breath. And then I told her everything. Quitting my job. Mary and Hannah and Quinton and the fight. And she listened with her brows gathered and her hand resting on mine.

"What are you going to do?"

"There's nothing to do. She's not coming back."

One brow rose. "And she told you this?"

I shook my head. "You don't understand."

"Enlighten me."

"Some things can't be mended, Katie. She lied to me about him."

"And you lied to her about Mary."

"Exactly. We're both wrong. We hurt each other, and the wound she hit in me is one I can't recover from. I don't … I want to trust her, but it was too close to home. You know, I never suspected Mary and Jack. Not even once, not for a second. I trusted her blindly. She hadn't even done anything to earn it. And Hannah did everything to earn it, but I couldn't give it to her. I'm ruined."

She shook her head, her eyes heavy and sad. "I don't want to believe it. I don't want to believe there's nothing you can do to get her back."

"I don't want to believe it either. But she's not coming back."

"Then go get her."

"It's a little too late for all that. She was right—I couldn't look her in the eye and tell her I believed her, not when it mattered."

"Do you?"

I ran a hand over my mouth. "She wouldn't have lied to me. I know she wouldn't have."

"And you don't think it's worth you telling her that? Sounds to me like you owe her an apology."

"I do. I just don't know how to or if she'll listen. And I don't know to what end. I'm not ready for this; I knew that much before it even got started. I knew I'd hurt her. I just didn't expect to get hurt too. And she walked away. She doesn't trust me either."

"So you've spent all weekend licking your wounds. Don't you think she's worth fighting for?"

Emotion blossomed in my chest. "Of course I do. She's the only woman I've ever felt the desire to fight for. I didn't fight for Mary, didn't even fight for our divorce. I didn't fight for my kids, not until Hannah, and all because I was afraid. I want to fight for her, but I don't know how. How do I fix this? There's nothing I can say to make it right. Katie, I want her back, but I'm afraid."

"Well, forgive me for saying so, but that's bullshit."

I opened my mouth to argue, but she cut me off. "Maybe it's time to do it anyway. Was quitting your job easy? No," she answered for me, "it wasn't. And neither was attending custody hearings and lawyer meetings and working as hard as you have to keep this house running. It wasn't easy for you to start staying home more, and it wasn't easy for you to help with the kids, but you did. It wasn't easy for you to trust Hannah, but you do. And you should. She wouldn't do anything to hurt you."

"And if I hurt her?"

"Well, that's a risk she'll have to choose to take or not to take. But don't use that as an excuse not to ask."

She watched me for a moment, searching my eyes, but she didn't find answers. I had none to offer.

So, having said her piece, she changed the subject. "What will you do about the children now that she's gone?"

"I'll keep Sammy in preschool, but after this month, I'll keep Maven home with me to save money—at least until I figure out what I'm going to do with myself. We have plenty to keep us afloat for a long while, especially if I sell the house."

Her face just kept getting sadder, and my heart just kept sinking.

"Well," she said after a second, "don't worry about me, all right? If you need to let me go, I don't want you to think twice. Because I'll be just fine."

I covered her hand with mine. "Thank you. Right now, I need all the help I can get."

Sammy appeared in the doorway with his hair standing up in every direction and eyes bright. "Hi, Katie!"

"Heya, bud," she said cheerily. "You hungry?"

He nodded. "Are there any more *poffertjes* left? Hannah made a big bag! Will she be back before they're gone, Daddy?"

I shook my head and tried to smile. "No, Sammy. Remember? Hannah went home."

His smile fell, his shoulders sloping. "Oh, yeah. Maybe I can draw her a picture. Can we send her a letter?"

I got out of my chair and moved to kneel in front of him. "I don't have her address, but if you want to write her, maybe I can find a way to get it to her, okay?"

He nodded at his bare feet. "'Kay. I just want to tell her we miss her. Maybe if we tell her we miss her, she'll come back."

I reached for my son and pulled him into my chest, my own aching and cracked and split open. "Maybe so," I said quietly before letting him go.

Katie fed Sammy while I woke Maven and dressed her, and an hour later, I dropped them off at school and headed home alone.

Even with Katie home, the house was too big and quiet. I made my way to my office, trying not to think about Hannah's empty room as I passed it, the door closed, as if it could keep the memories inside. But it was no use.

The office felt foreign, full of books that no longer held value. I sat in the chair that had been part of another life. And I stared at the open doorway, unsure of my future.

It was too much, that room. I picked up my laptop and walked out, closing the door behind me.

There was no escaping any of it.

The best I could do in the way of a distraction was to pester Katie in the kitchen while she folded towels. We chatted about nothing while I browsed real estate, trying to get a handle on what I could ask for the house and what I could get that was smaller, more modest, less empty, and without the memories this place held.

It was just before lunch when the doorbell rang.

I opened the door expecting a package, but I found Lysanne instead, her jaw set and eyes hard.

"Hannah asked me to bring you this," she said before I even had a chance to greet her, thrusting an envelope at me.

I took it and stepped out of the way. "Please, come in."

She sighed as she walked past me and into the entryway.

"Is she all right?" I asked.

"No, she isn't."

I took a breath and cleared my throat. "What's this?"

"Open it and see for yourself."

I watched her for a second, my mind full of questions my mouth wouldn't speak, long enough for her to fold her arms and nod to the envelope in my hand.

So I opened it up, unprepared for the wash of emotions that hit me when I saw what was inside.

First, a letter addressed to the children in Hannah's handwriting, the long slant of her letters elegant and easy.

Sammy and Maven,

It's time for me to go home. I loved every day I spent with you and all the fun we had while baking and playing and singing together. I'll miss you both very much, and I'll think of you all the time, I know it. I've written my address here. Will you send me letters? I'll send you letters back.

I'm so sorry I wasn't able to say goodbye and give you both one last hug, but wrap your arms around yourself very, very tight. Close your eyes and squeeze. And remember me. I won't forget you.

—Hannah

My heart thudded against my ribs, my throat squeezing tight, tighter still when I saw the address she'd written below was in Holland.

My eyes snapped to Lysanne's, who was still watching me with irritation.

"She's gone back to the Netherlands?" I breathed, disbelieving, and stepped over to the bench to sink into it.

She nodded once. "You didn't expect her to stay after all that, did you?"

"Well … yes. Yes, I did. I … I didn't even realize that was on the table."

I looked down at my hands, flipping to the page behind the letter. She'd drawn a picture of her and the kids in the park with a rainbow overhead, perfectly lovely, perfectly happy.

And I realized there was something in the bottom of the envelope and reached in.

It was a Polaroid of her and the kids that she'd taken herself, the three of them smiling and smushed into the frame. I touched the image of her face with my thumb.

"I …" My throat closed; I swallowed the words.

"She left Friday for home. I tried to get her to stay, tried to get her to call you, but it was no use."

My eyes were still on the photo in my hand. "I can't believe she's gone."

"Well, I can't believe you believed Quinton over her. Of all the things. She didn't tell you about him, which I understand upsets you, but she had her reasons, the first being that Quinton had nothing to do with you and the second being that it hurts her to speak of it."

"What happened between them?"

"That's not my story to tell." She took a seat next to me. "She never would have hurt you, Charlie. She is the most loving, loyal, giving person I have ever known in my life, and you accused her of the unthinkable. That is, *after* your *wife* confronted her, hurt her. And then you delivered the final blow. And now, she's gone. She ran all the way back home, ran away to be where she's safe, and it's your fault."

"I know," I said miserably and ran a hand along my unshaven jaw. "I know. And there's nothing I can do about it. She was right. My heart and my soul are tangled up and used up and broken, and I can't love her like she deserves. I have too much hanging over me to give her what I wish I could."

Her cheeks flamed. "That's not at all true. You're here, wounded and pouting, sad over her, but there's plenty you can do. You're broken, yes, but she loves you. She loves you, and she'll care for you. And you know she can. You know she can heal anything; it's her magic."

"But she's gone. She's not coming back."

Lysanne leaned toward me. "Then make her come back. You're the only one who can. You need to talk to her. You need to tell her you're sorry and how you feel, or you're going to lose her forever."

"Haven't I already?" I asked, my voice rough.

"No, I don't believe you have. But you've got to apologize, and you've got to listen to her. Prove to her you'll be what she deserves because she deserves everything. And I think you can give it to her. You just have to decide to maybe comb your hair and have a good shave and do something about it."

I blinked at her, my mind stumbling over what she'd said.

The truth was, I owed Hannah so much more than an apology. Deep down, I realized I'd been holding out hope that it somehow wasn't over. Geographically, I'd thought she was around the corner, but instead, she'd gone halfway across the world to get away from me.

Lysanne was right. And there was only one thing I could do about it.

I only hoped Lysanne was right.

Because if there was a chance, I'd take it.

HANNAH

When my phone rang, *his* name was the last I'd expected to see on my screen. I stared at my phone for a long, breathless second, my eyes on his name, before ducking out of the kitchen under watchful eyes and accepting the call.

"Hello, Charlie," I answered softly, sadly.

"Hannah," he said, the depths of his feelings in one breath, one word, two syllables—my name. "I … I got your letter."

I stepped outside and closed the door behind me, sitting on the stoop, saying nothing.

"I'm sorry," he whispered. "I want you to know, I'm sorry. For what I said, for what I didn't say."

"So am I."

He paused. I didn't speak.

"I … I want you to understand … I want to explain. When I saw you with *him*, when he said what he said, I didn't believe him. In my heart, I didn't believe him. In my soul, I knew better. But my mind told me I'd been there before. You have to understand that, when faced with the thought of him and you, my brain rang a warning. And I know that's not fair. I know too well what Mary has done to me and what I've lost because of it. I told you before we started this that I'd hurt you, and I did. I told you I was broken, and I am."

"I know. I know why you're hurt, and I understand why you felt what you felt. And I'm sorry too, for not telling you about him and for not trusting you about Mary." I propped my elbows on my knees, my eyes on the elm in front of the house, the pattern of the bark like a maze. "Charlie, Quinton and I didn't sleep together."

"I know. I believe you."

"But he wanted to."

Silence.

I took a deep, painful breath. "He wouldn't leave me alone, not from the minute I walked through their door. The night before I left, he came into my room while I was sleeping, and he … he …" I swallowed. "When I woke, his hands were on me, and he was kissing me. But he didn't do what he could have done, and he left when I told him to. The next morning, I quit."

"Hannah ..." The word was thick and heavy with pain.

"He found me somehow; I know that now after he admitted he saw us together. He'd been following me, I think. The first time it seemed like it might have been a coincidence. The second time, I didn't believe him. I wanted to tell you then, but ... Charlie, you're not the only one who's afraid. I thought you might believe this was something I had done. And that's exactly what you ended up thinking. I should have just told you from the start."

"No, don't do that. I'm sorry. I'm so sorry. And I ... I accused you of ... God, Hannah."

My eyes filled with tears.

"Did you file a report? Tell me you did."

I shook my head, forgetting he couldn't see me. "No. I left the country. He can't hurt me here."

He swore under his breath. "There might still be a way. Will you let me look into it? Because we might be able to prosecute. We could—"

"Charlie, please," I said gently. "It's all right."

"It's not all right. Nothing about this is all right."

"But it is. As much as I hate all of this, it's okay. Because you and I felt right and good, but it wasn't the right time, not for either of us. But I don't belong there; I never did. I wish I could have only worked for you. I wish I could have helped you, but I only complicated things. I only made it harder."

"No," he said, his voice rough. "You did help me. You made everything better, not worse. I want you back. Tell me what I have to do. I want you to come home, Hannah."

"I *am* home. Charlie, don't you understand? Your life ... your life is too complicated, too crowded for me, don't you see? My being there caused Mary so much pain that she put Maven's and Sammy's safety at risk. My being there complicates you being able to sort through your divorce, your job—"

"I quit my job, Hannah."

I paused. "You what?"

"I quit the day you left me. I came home to tell you, but you were picking up the kids. And when I went to meet you, I saw you with him."

I took a shaky breath, a pregnant pause. "What will you do?" I finally asked.

"I don't know. I just know I don't want to be away from home anymore. I don't want to be away from you. But now … now, you're gone. I thought … I hoped for a second that it wasn't real—this feeling that it was over," he said, the words breaking.

My breath hitched, my words trembling as hot tears rolled down my cheeks. "I wish things had been different. I wish the timing had been better. And now, it's too late. Charlie, this is the right thing," I insisted. "You're still married. You have Mary to sort out and your children who need you. And I need some time. I just need time."

"Will time change your mind?"

"Maybe. But I can't come back. I can't. I shouldn't have ever left in the first place. But for a moment, I had you, and that made it worth the pain."

He didn't speak; the silence was oppressive.

"I want nothing but happiness for you," I said. "And I hope you find it. I know you will."

"Not without you," he whispered.

"You will. I know it."

Put like that, he didn't refuse. "Hannah, I … I don't know what to say."

I swallowed the stone in my throat. "I think this is where we say goodbye."

He didn't say anything for a long moment where the wind blew the oak so its branches creaked and rustled.

"I'm sorry I couldn't be everything you deserve," he finally said.

"And I'm sorry I couldn't save you." My breath hitched, my tears silent, and when I found my voice, I said words that broke me completely because I knew I'd never hear his voice again. "Goodbye, Charlie."

CHARLIE

I cupped my hand over my mouth, elbows on my knees, the ache in my chest deep and burning.

The revelation of what he'd done to her, of what *I'd* done to her, was almost too much to bear. I hurt her far worse than I could have imagined, believing him over her, and after what he'd done. But I'd done so much worse by not taking her side, by not trusting her when it mattered most.

I couldn't look past myself to see the truth of her.

I had to make it up to her. I couldn't give up. Not without fighting for her.

And I knew exactly what to do. I only hoped she would take me back.

Letting Go

HANNAH

Music played from the portable speaker, the overhead light shining down on the long countertop in the center of the room, which was covered in flour, and my hands were kneading dough, squeezing and folding it and squeezing it again.

The bakery had closed an hour before, and Mama had gone home, leaving Annelise and me to finish preparations for the next morning. I was in charge of the dough, and Annelise was busy soaking grains and berries and leaven for our breads.

I had spent my childhood in this kitchen with the smell of sugar and yeast and sweet vanilla and cinnamon. I'd fallen asleep as a little girl under the table to the sounds of the women of my family talking and laughing and gossiping and sharing their lives with each other. I'd sat on my *opa*'s lap and helped him roll *banketstaaf* and chased my baby brothers around the counter and under the feet of our family.

This place was just as much my home as the house where we

lived. Maybe more.

Days had passed since Charlie called, and I didn't find myself much closer to finding peace or comfort. Not with the finality of what we'd said, not with the thousands of miles I'd put between us.

I had a feeling it would be a very long time before my heart healed. And in the meantime, I would bake and lose myself in the bustling business of my family.

It seemed the only thing to do.

"Have you heard from him again?" Annelise asked, reading my mind, breaking the silence.

"No," I answered, grateful for the fact that he hadn't tried to call again in equal measure to the hurt I felt that he hadn't.

"Do you think you will?"

"No, I don't." I paused, flipping the dough, eyes on my hands. "It's over. We said goodbye. And my only consolation is that it's behind me. I don't know if I could have withstood him if he hadn't let me go, if he hadn't given up."

"So if he put up a fight, you would bend?"

"I don't know. I don't want to know."

She made a noise. "I don't believe that."

Hurt flashed through me. "No, I suppose I don't really either. I miss him. I miss the children and Katie and … I just miss it all. For a moment, I made a life for myself, and I lost it almost in the same breath. But I'm home now; I fit here in a way I don't fit anywhere else."

Annelise dried her hands, searching my face. "You didn't fit with Charlie?"

I didn't meet her eyes. "I thought maybe I could. But I don't belong there, Annelise. That life wasn't mine, and it never could be. I wanted Charlie's heart before he was free to give it to me, when it was still damaged, when it hadn't yet healed."

"Only bad timing. Is that right?"

"It was bad timing, but it was the right time. I think … I think he needed me. And I wish more than anything that things had been different, but they're not. It's no one's fault."

"It's all so final," she said, "so desolate. How can you be so … I don't know. Calm? Accepting? Don't you want to fight? Don't you want to try to change your fate?"

Knead and fold, knead and fold, the dough cold and supple in my hands. "How can I fight something I can't change? The things I want aren't in my reach. If they were, they would be in my hands."

"Like the bakery?"

"Yes," I answered quietly. "Like the bakery."

She moved to my side, leaning back against the table to face me. "Hannah, I wish things were different."

"I know. So do I."

"It was all decided before we were even born. I almost wish it had been you, but I love it too."

"I know that, too. And so it's inevitable. Do you understand? I can only take what's offered."

"And Charlie's not on offer?"

I sighed. "He wants to be, but Annelise … his wife, she wants … she wants things she can't have too. And she'll hurt me to get to him. She'll use the children to hurt him, hurt him even more than she already has. And I want to help him. I want to save him."

I laid my hands on the floured surface of the table and finally looked up.

"Maybe it was hasty to leave so soon. Maybe I should have stayed. But after everything, when he accused me, when he said he didn't know if he could trust me, I was too hurt to stay. It all tallied up, all the ways we couldn't be together, and I left. And now, I can't go back. I don't want to go back, not when everything there is hard and unfamiliar and foreign. But I wish … I wish for a great many things that I'll never have. And I only know that I belong *here*, not there."

Her eyes were sad and soft, her own wish to change things written on her face. "I'm sorry," she said.

"So am I."

"What will you do now?"

"Well, for the time, I'll fold dough and bake and hide here where it's safe and warm, where I can heal. And then … then I don't know. Teach maybe."

"Maybe you could teach Oma some manners."

I laughed. "It's not possible. She lost them long before you or me."

Annelise's brows rose. "You think she ever had them?"

I shrugged. "Mama seems to think so."

"Has Oma cornered you to tell her about Charlie yet?"

"I've somehow found a way to avoid her, but she'll catch me at some point, I know it. She's fast for an old lady."

"Very nimble. Maybe if you make sure she's had plenty of wine at *Sinterklaas*, it'll slow her down."

I laughed. "And me be responsible for her breaking a hip? No, thank you."

"Well, let me know if you want me to help run interference. I'm glad to get her good and drunk—or at the very least keep her occupied. Maybe I'll even let her teach me to knit; she's only been trying to convince me to learn since I was six."

"Oh God." I chuckled. "You really do love me."

And she smiled, pulling me in for a hug. "I really do, Hannah. And I'm glad you're home."

"So am I," I said, wishing the words were true.

CHARLIE

What are you going to do about it, Charlie?

The answer was anything. Everything. Whatever I could.

It was the answer at my back as I walked into the hospital, a dozen speeches cycling through my anxious mind.

When I stepped off the elevator, I scanned the hall for Mary without finding what I was looking for. The nurses at the station eyed me as I asked for her, promising me they'd page her. And so I took a seat and waited, not sure if she'd come.

She did.

Her back was straight and jaw set, her body tight and arms folded across her chest.

I stood as she approached.

"What do you want?" she asked.

"Can we talk? Somewhere private?"

She watched me for a moment before nodding. "Come with me."

I followed her down the hallway, past the watchful eyes of the nurses, and to the empty on-call room.

The door closed behind us, and we stood a few feet away from each other, neither of us speaking.

She crossed her arms. "Well?"

"What do you want from me?" I asked harder than I meant to.

Her face tightened. "For starters, I want access to the kids."

"When you waive your rights to them, you can have that."

"You want me to give them up so I can have them?" she scoffed. "That's ludicrous, Charlie."

"It's not. How can I agree to let you see them when you're unreliable, unstable? When you won't follow the rules? If you want to see them, you've got to prove you're not going to *use* them."

She glared at me across the space between us. "If you won't give them to me, I'll fight for them."

"Let me paint that picture for you," I said, the words cold. "Let's say you fight me, and let's say you win. You'll have them at least half of the time and completely on your own. Every bath and every meal, every bedtime story and every load of laundry. You don't want that. Admit you don't want that. You don't want me or the kids or any of this. So, what *do* you want?"

Her jaw flexed, her eyes shining. "I want my life back."

My anger flared. I raked my hand through my hair to give myself a second to temper it. "Mary, how the hell do you suggest you get it back? What do you *want* from me? What am I supposed to do? You took the kids without telling me. You showed up after months of silence and expect everything. *You left us.*"

"*You* threw me out!"

"Because *you* fucked my best friend! Jesus Christ, how am *I* the bad guy here?"

"Well, you seemed to have moved on just fine. How's your pretty nanny?"

"She's gone." The words were hollow and desolate.

She rolled her eyes. "Don't look so sad. I'm sure you can just hire another one, can't you? Do you have to pay extra for blow jobs?"

That flare of anger caught fire, stoked by a painful wind in my ribs, rushing through my veins with every beat of my heart, and I exploded. *"You did this!"* I screamed. "Don't you understand? Don't you see what you've done to me? You've *ruined* me. I've made mistakes, God knows I've made mistakes, but if you hadn't treated me this way—lying, cheating, manipulating me, hurting me over and over again—if it wasn't for you, I wouldn't be broken, suspicious, looking for ways she might have betrayed me. I wouldn't have lost her if I'd been whole."

Mary stood very still, her eyes very wide, her lips parted slightly. "You love her."

"I love her, and I shouldn't have let you dictate my future. I love her, and I should have trusted her. And I should have worked harder to keep her away from you. But I can't change that any more than you can change the fact that you slept with Jack or that you abandoned us." I paused, looking her over, catching my breath, and with honesty and surrender in my broken voice, I asked her again, "What do you want, Mary?"

"I want to go back," she said, the words trembling and worn.

"Well, you can't. You didn't love me, and you don't now. Our lives, that life you miss—that life was a lie."

"But that's the closest I've ever gotten to real." Tears shone in her eyes, and she looked away. With a shaking breath, she sat on the edge of one of the beds. "I'm sorry. I'm fucked up, Charlie. I know I'm fucked up. When I left, I lost everything—my home, my husband, my family, my *place*. And, for all the time since then, I dealt with it by not dealing at all. I shut down. I worked. I ate. I slept. Until I saw *her* here with you, with Maven, in my place. And something in me snapped."

Her shoulders drooped, her face heavy with exhaustion, the fight washed out of her.

"I went right back to the way I'd always been because I didn't know what else to do, how else to fight. I wanted my old life back, and that was the moment I realized it. And every time you told me no, it only made me push harder."

I took a seat next to her, the bed dipping under my added weight. "I don't want to tell you no. I don't want to keep you from the kids. But I'm not going to give them to someone who will hurt them. I won't."

"I know. That's why they're better off with you."

My chest tightened with exaltation and sorrow. "If you follow the rules, you can see them. You can see them sooner than later if you waive your rights. It's the only way I'll know you're not going to fight me back. And I need you to let that old life go. Because there's no going back—only forward. You're the only one who can make the choice to let go so we can all move on."

Mary sighed. "The nanny said something when I saw her last, something I can't stop thinking about. She said she didn't want to hurt me, that none of you did. But I wanted to hurt you. I wanted to hurt her, and I can't really tell you why."

"Do you still?"

She thought about it, eyes on her hands clasped between her knees. "It didn't make me happy, and it didn't get me what I wanted. Like you said, there's no going back, especially given the fact that you're in love with your nanny."

"Hannah. She hasn't been the nanny in a long while."

"And if I sign the waiver, if I follow your rules, I can see the kids?"

"Anytime you want," I promised and meant it.

She nodded at the ground and met my eyes. "Tell me what I need to do, and I'll do it."

So I did.

To Belong

HANNAH

The night was cold with the smell of snow in the air, and our fireplace was crackling and warm. We all sat in the living room, the couches and chairs and floor space taken other than the middle of the room where the youngest of the family skipped around in circles. All of us sang, all fifteen of us—my entire family.

It was December 5th, and *Sinterklaas* would come that night. We'd eaten until we were ready to burst and settled into the living room with coffee and cookies and singing. Any moment, the doorbell would ring—my uncle had already slipped out with the gifts to leave on the stoop. And then we would all open our presents and poems.

My cousin started "The Wind Keeps Blowing," and as my family sang in a chorus of voices, I felt tears sting my nose and eyes, my throat squeezing the words to a whisper, the familiarity of the moment and the longing in my heart a combination that swept me under.

Through the trees, the wind keeps blowing,
In our homes, we sense its might.
Will the Holy Saint keep going?
Will he make it through the night?
Will he make it through the night?

Yes, he overcomes the darkness,
On his horse, so fierce and fast.
When he learns we long for his presence,
The Good Saint will come at last.
The Good Saint will come at last.

As our voices died, the doorbell rang. The children ran screaming for the door with all of us on their heels, and when Coen and Bas threw the door open, I stopped so suddenly, Johanna ran into me and Mama ran into her and Oma ran into her.

Charlie stood on the step of the house looking tired and confused and hopeful, scanning the faces in the threshold until he found mine and held my eyes, sending a shock of relief through me in a beat of my heart.

We all stared at Charlie with our mouths hanging open, and he stood there, staring back, all of us stunned silent.

Until my brother broke the silence.

"Who are you?" Bas asked, accusing.

Charlie looked down at him. "I'm sorry … I, uh … do you speak English?"

The twins turned back to look at us, completely dumbfounded.

I found myself and stepped forward. "Charlie? What … what are you doing here?"

He took a breath — I thought he might have been petrified for a moment from the shock.

"Hannah, I …" He swallowed hard.

"Go on and say it," Oma said impatiently.

We all turned to look at her, a few surprised laughs rolling through us.

My mama turned to her. "Come on, Mama, everybody." She directed the crowd back from the door, offering me an encouraging nod.

I stepped out onto the stoop where I'd said goodbye to him a few days before, the stoop where he now stood with hopeful, worried eyes.

"Charlie, what … how …" I stammered, unable to formulate sentences or coherent thought.

"There's too much to say. I had to come here and say it. I have to tell you what you mean to me without thousands of miles between us."

And when I looked into his eyes, I knew I was lost.

"When Mary left, my life fell apart, and I found that everything I'd thought I'd known about who I was and what I wanted was a lie. When you walked into that broken life of mine, I learned that life could be so much more than it was. When I saw you with him, when he said what he said, I was too broken to see the truth when it mattered most. And when you left me, I knew I had to try to get you back."

"Charlie," I breathed, "I—"

"Please," he begged, "don't say no. Not yet."

I nodded, and he continued. "I don't know how to tell you that you saved me. Because when I met you, I was a shadow, a shade of the man I'd once wanted to be. But you shone your light on me and showed me what I could be, what I wanted. You gave me the courage to reach out and take what I wanted, and I betrayed that gift by not standing by you. And I could give you a thousand excuses, but none of them would absolve me of the wrong I've done.

"I don't know how to tell you that I'm sorry. Because I should have believed every word you said. I knew in my heart that you would never lie, and I knew in the depths of my soul that you would never hurt me. But I'd used up all my trust on someone who abused it, and when you needed me, I abandoned you, just like I'd been abandoned. I hurt you just like I'd been hurt.

"But what I do know is that I love you. I love you for the way you have filled my life with joy, for the kindness and grace you breathe into everything you do. I love you for showing me what kind of man I want to be—a man who could deserve someone like you. I love you, and I'm sorry. And if you'll forgive me, I'll spend every day and every breath proving it to you."

He took a step closer, his eyes full of love and adoration and hope. "I *do* trust you, Hannah. I was just hurt and afraid—afraid of losing you, afraid of loving you. I was wrong, and you were right about everything except one thing. You do belong. You belong with me, and I belong to you. Home isn't home, not without you."

He paused, and I breathed, and we looked into each other's eyes in silence.

"Kiss her, you fool!" Oma said eagerly, leaning out of the open window next to us.

"Mama!" I heard my mother scold, grabbing her by the shoulders to pull her back in.

But I laughed, tears in my eyes as Charlie smiled down at me.

"I do love you, Hannah. I love you more than I knew I could. I need you more than I believed was possible. Come home. Please, come back to me."

I closed the small distance between us, touched his chest, looked into the depths of his eyes, not knowing what to say.

He touched my cheek, held my face, pleading. "I only want to make you happy. I only want to give you all of me—my heart, my life, my love. Will you let me?"

And the truth of my heart was all I could hear, all I could speak, just one word, a word I'd once wished for from his lips that he now wished from mine. And I gave it to him.

I would give him anything.

"Yes."

A relieved sound escaped him, a laugh or a sob that puffed against my lips just before he kissed them, sealing his promise, sealing my fate, searing his name on my heart.

I barely heard the cheers of my family behind me, too lost in his arms and mouth and lips as we twisted together, still hanging on to each other as the kiss ended.

He pressed his forehead to mine, his eyes closed. "I'm sorry," he whispered. "Forgive me."

"I do," I whispered back. "I love you," I said, that simple fact absolving us both.

And he kissed me again with the promise of forever on his lips.

CHARLIE

Hannah in my arms was all I'd ever want for as long as I lived. I knew it then. I'd known it always.

I reluctantly let her go, and she leaned into me as the door opened behind her.

We turned to her chattering family.

"Everyone," Hannah said, "this is Charlie. Charlie, meet my family."

They all spoke at once, reaching for me. Her mother kissed my cheeks, hers high and rosy. Her father clasped my hand with a strong grip and a warm smile, and her sisters took turns kissing my cheeks too, three times on alternating sides. Her little oma was next, nearly pushing one of her cousins out of the way to get to me.

"Come here," she said, her hands up and open, reaching for my face.

I obliged, bending over for her to reach me and kiss my cheeks, too. But she held me there instead of letting me go.

"I can see why she didn't want to talk about you. I would have told her she was being stupid."

I laughed. "Well, I'm glad I would have had your support."

"Yes, well, I am old enough to know when you have something to lose that you'll regret not going after. But tell me, Charlie—you came all the way here for her, but if you take her away, will you treat her with care?"

"I swear it," I said, my voice low and serious.

She patted my cheek and smiled. "You're a good boy. You take care of her."

"I will."

"You'd better."

"Come on, Mama," Hannah's mother said, shaking her head apologetically at me.

I met her aunt, uncle, cousins and her younger brothers. Everyone was so blond and so tall, I felt almost like I was a normal height.

The crowd filtered into the living room, and Hannah ushered me in to sit in an armchair. She sat on the arm, leaning into me, her arm around my shoulders.

"Where are the children?" she asked me as everyone was getting settled.

"My mom came up from Florida after I figured out what to do. I couldn't … I couldn't let you go. I'm sorry I didn't listen."

"I'm not," she said softly and kissed my temple. "Let's just stay for a little while. Can we go somewhere?"

My arm slipped around her waist, my hand coming to rest on her thigh. "Of course. There's so much I want to say, so much more. I just … I can't believe I'm here and that you said yes."

She brushed my hair from my forehead. "All I've ever wanted to say is yes, Charlie."

Hannah kissed me gently, chastely, and all I wanted to do was pull her into my lap and hold her and kiss her and love her.

Her uncle ducked out with a wink, and everyone began to sing a cheery song in Dutch, the whole lot of them. A few of them harmonized, the sound so lovely, I felt nostalgic without even understanding what they said.

The doorbell rang a moment later, and this time when the children opened it, it was to a sack of presents. The twins dragged the velvet bag in by its rope like they were hauling a twenty-point buck, and when they opened it, they took turns passing out the contents. There was a gift for everyone—everyone but me, of course, but I already had my gift. There was quite literally nothing else I could have asked for.

They opened their presents one at a time. Every present had a poem or letter attached to it, and they read them aloud—Hannah translated for me. Most of them were jokes or teased the recipient, and every one seemed to have meaning, nothing extravagant, all of them thoughtful.

And just like that, I had an idea.

But not for tonight. Tonight, all I wanted was Hannah.

We ate pastries and drank coffee and talked and answered a thousand questions until Hannah disappeared to pack, giving me plenty of time to pull Oma over and enlist her help, ending up enlisting both of her sisters and mother too, because there were apparently no secrets in that house. And just as we finalized our plan, Hannah returned with a small bag to take my hand again. And we said goodbye to her family with promises to see each other the next day.

The second the door closed, I pulled her into me and kissed her. I kissed her as the snow began to fall, the warmth of her a part of me, our breath mingling. I kissed her and told her how much I loved her, and I hoped she understood.

"I can't believe you're here," she said when she pulled away.

"It was the only thing left to do, the only way I knew to prove that I meant it when I said I wanted you back." I kissed her again, just once, and took her bag. "Plus, I had Lysanne at my back with a pitchfork."

She laughed down at her feet as we walked. "Yes, she would do that."

"It helped that she was right. I owe you so much, more than I can ever repay you for, more than I can ever give you. More than I deserve."

She pulled me to a stop on the sidewalk. "Why don't you feel that you deserve me?"

I watched her face in the moonlight, the snow whispering around us. "Because you're everything right, everything good. Because everything you touch is made better. But everything I touch spoils. You're young and beautiful and *free*. And I wish I could have always belonged to you and you alone."

"Are you mine now?"

I stepped closer. "Hannah, I'm yours for as long as you'll have me. I'm yours even if you don't want me. My heart was in your hands the first moment I saw your face."

"Then it isn't about what we think we deserve. It's about honoring what's been given to us. I promise to honor your love if you'll honor mine."

"I will," I breathed, stepping into her. "I do."

And I sealed the vow with a kiss in the falling snow.

We hurried to the hotel a few blocks away and up the stairs and to my room. The building was old, but the interior had been remodeled, though they'd left the original fireplace —when she ducked into the bathroom, I built a fire. And then I turned out the lights, kicking off my shoes and hanging up my coat, climbing into bed to wait for her.

When she opened the door, she stepped out and walked through the quiet room.

Hannah was an angel in white, with alabaster skin and hair the color of wheat, her eyes like sea glass, clear and blue and deep and fixed on me. The fire cast the gauzy fabric in an orange glow, her body a silhouette, but I could see every curve, see the shadows of her breasts and her peaked nipples, the valley of her waist and the swell of her hips.

And when she was at my side, when she was in my arms, when her breath was my own, I found myself no longer free.

I didn't want to be free. I only wanted to be hers.

My hands held her face in the firelight, held her body against mine, laid her down, her hair spread out around her like gold. Down her body I moved, her legs parting and thighs shifting against my thighs, then my waist, my hands wanting to touch all of her. They slipped up her legs, taking her nightgown with it until it was hitched over her waist, but my eyes were down, at the center of her, which was where I wanted to touch most of all.

I settled between her thighs, opening them up, my breath ragged as my fingers spread her open, and I lowered my lips, closing my mouth over her core.

A sigh slipped out of her at the contact, her hands twisting into my hair when I swept my tongue, thighs trembling when I slipped my finger into her heat, and I took my time, waiting until her hips rolled and breath grew loud. And then I let her go, backed off the bed, stood with the fire at my back and reached between my shoulder blades to grab my shirt and tug it over my head.

I gripped my belt as she watched me with heavy lids and swollen lips, her legs still spread and hips shifting gently. I unfastened my pants and stepped out of them, climbed up her body, pushing her nightgown up her ribs, over her breasts. She moved to pull it over her head, and before it was even gone, my fingers were grazing her long neck, her collarbone. The weight of her breast rested in my palm, her nipple tight under my circling thumb, her lips parted, her eyes on my own. And I lowered my mouth to hers as her fingers closed around my length, her hips angling until my crown rested against her core.

I flexed my hips, sliding into her gently as my tongue searched her mouth with slow purpose. And when I had filled her, when there was no space between us, skin to skin, heart to heart, I was whole. I was home.

We moved together, her arms around my neck, my hand gripping her thigh, our bodies a wave and lips never parting, not until she turned her head, her eyes pinched shut, whispering my name as I pumped faster, harder. Her neck arched, her chin pointing at the ceiling, a gasp of pleasure that marked a shuddering throb through her when she came, and I was right behind her, letting my past go with the future in my arms.

Dreamers

HANNAH

I woke the next morning tangled up in Charlie, aching and sore in all the best ways.

For a long time, I lay there awake in his arms, listening to his heart beat and his slow breath, wondering over my future, not the least bit afraid.

He'd shown me the waiver, told me that Mary had let him and the children go. He'd told me again what I'd always known—that he did trust me, that he did love me—and I knew he'd never second-guess me again. We'd talked about Quinton through my tears, and I didn't doubt for a breath that Charlie would never forgive himself for not believing me.

But we hadn't talked about what would come, though I knew he'd want me to come back with him, and I knew I'd go.

There were no more questions. Everything had been stripped down to its simplest form—I wanted him, and he wanted me.

After a while, he woke, his hands finding my hair and his lips finding mine, almost as if they needed to be certain I was real. And the kiss deepened with our breath, our bodies finding their way together again.

We spent the morning in bed, only deciding to leave when we were too hungry to stay where we were. So we showered and dressed, walked along the canal until we found a café for brunch, and ate bread and jam and cheese until we were satisfied.

And then we headed back to my parents' house. I popped my head in just to ask to borrow their bikes and a blanket and basket, which brought everyone out to talk to us. But an hour later, after stopping by the market, we were sitting on a plaid blanket, sipping wine and eating more bread and more cheese.

Charlie took a bite of cheese, stretched out on the blanket next to me, the wind ruffling his hair as he looked across the field and toward the green pastures beyond. The snow hadn't stuck, and the day was bright and sunny and crisp and perfect. I looked in the same direction with a sigh.

"So beautiful," he said.

"It really is, isn't it?"

"The countryside is nice too."

I smiled down at him, touching his face as I kissed him, running my thumb over his bottom lip when I pulled away.

"I've got something for you." He moved for his bag as I watched, curious.

And when I saw what was in his hands, I was too stunned to speak.

He handed me the wooden shoe, stuffed to the brim, painted with a scene of a bakery with a pink-striped awning and a sign that read *Lekker*, and along the edge were the words, *Home is where the heart is*, in Dutch. I touched the words and met his twinkling eyes.

"Charlie ..."

"Look inside."

So I did. Inside were rolled up drawings from Sammy and Maven and a snowflake they'd made for me out of popsicle sticks. My curiosity rose when I found Oma's set of silver measuring spoons nestled in the bed of hay, coming to a roll of paper last, tied with a broad red ribbon.

I set the shoe down and untied the ribbon, the paper unfurling to reveal a real estate listing.

My hands went numb. It was the sandwich shop near Charlie's house, and behind it was an unsigned lease agreement.

My eyes snapped to his, and he sat up.

"I've been thinking about what I want to do with my life since you left me, and I knew without a doubt that I wanted to be with you and that I didn't want to go back to law. And when I thought about being with you, it made me want my family, want that future I'd dreamed of. It made me wonder why I had to find another job. It made me wonder if I could help you have your dream so that I could have mine."

He looked down at the papers in my hands, but my gaze stayed on his long face, on his elegant nose and the curves of his lips.

"You have the ability and skill to run a bakery, and I have the money to put behind it and the business acumen to help you run it. The apartment above the shop was for lease too, and I've got everything ready to list my house and take this lease. I can stay home with the kids, and you can have your bakery. And it would be yours. The papers have already been drawn up, and everything is in your name. If something happens, if I lose you again, if I lose you for good, the shop is yours."

I swallowed back tears, and he took my hand.

"Hannah, just say the word. Say the word, and it's yours. If you need time to think—"

"Yes," I blurted, the word tight with emotion and my cheeks hot.

He searched my face, his voice hushed. "Are you sure? Don't ... I know I put you on the spot with all of this, and I—"

I shut him up with a kiss, rising up on my knees as his arms wound around my waist.

When I broke away, he looked up at me with a lazy, hazy smile.

"You bought me a bakery," I said with wonder.

He shrugged. "I'm only in it for the *kwarktaart*."

And I laughed against his lips and kissed him again, knowing dreams were free and feeling like the luckiest woman in the world because every one of mine had come true.

Epilogue

CHARLIE

two years later...

E verything smelled like apples.

The scent hung in the air of the apartment, as much a part of it as the couch or the table or the rocking chair where I sat, rocking Ava, her bottom so little, it fit in the palm of my hand. She was only a month old, and she smelled like apples too, apples and milk and *baby*—that intoxicating concoction that made you feel your mortality as surely as it made you feel infinite.

It was early—the sun had just begun to lighten the sky, and the birds had yet to wake and begin their chirping. Maven and Sammy would still be asleep for another hour at least, and Hannah was already downstairs in the bakery with Fein—her cousin who had recently moved from Holland—getting ready for the day. With *appelflappen*, if I had to guess. It had become the shop's bestseller over the last couple of months, per my numbers, maybe because of fall's entrance or the upcoming holidays. Or maybe because Hannah's cooking was actual magic, and people just couldn't get enough.

I'd bank on that being the truth, and I could attest to the fact that Hannah was in fact magic.

We'd spent the last two years building the shop and building our lives together, the two of us finding easy symmetry and harmony. The weekend after my divorce was final, Hannah and I had flown with the kids to Holland and were married. And no one had told us we were rushing, and no one had accused us of being crazy.

It seemed everyone who truly cared for us knew as well as we did that we were meant for each other.

Mary had done as I'd asked, and at first, she'd tried. She had occasionally called and asked to see the kids, but those calls had become few and far between until they'd stopped all together. And Quinton had been charged and ended up on probation, with a divorce and a restraining order to boot. We hadn't seen him again.

Construction on the bakery had been stressful and long, but when we'd opened, business had taken off. The sandwich shop had always done all right, but *Lekker* was such a welcome neighborhood addition that it had become a staple, the place everyone would go to for coffee and pastries in the morning, where they would work at the big table facing the window, just like Hannah had imagined. Within six months, we had been in the black.

And I might well be in heaven.

Don't get me wrong; being a stay-at-home dad was weird and disorienting and made me feel like I'd lost some part of myself, lost my identity. But it was also everything I had wanted. I got to coach Sammy's little league team and attend Maven's ballet recital, which was really just an adorable cat herding of a dozen five-year-olds in tutus. The day-to-day monotony of raising small children was balanced by the feeling of rightness, the understanding that I was where I needed to be, where I wanted to be. And I had been able to help Hannah build something we were both proud of, give her her dream just like I'd wanted. She'd already made all mine come true.

I hummed "Hey Jude," rubbing Ava's back as I rocked her. It was my favorite time of day—when the world was asleep, my baby was in my arms, my wife was downstairs doing what she loved, and the day was full of possibility and promise. It was the first thing I did every day, before coffee, before anything. I would sit in this chair and hold my daughter as I considered just how fortunate I was.

Ava wriggled, her arms stretching over her head and tiny fists balled up, nuzzling her face into my shoulder, rooting around for something she wasn't likely to get from me.

"Come on. You want Mama?"

She mewled a little cry, and I smiled as I stood and shuffled down the building's stairs in my slippers, sleep pants, and a hoodie—my uniform.

Hannah stood behind the cases, loading them with trays of pastries with little chalkboard signs, looking as blissfully happy as I felt, if not a little tired. She waved, and Fein ran around to unlock the front door for me.

I stepped into the warm shop as Hannah walked around the counter, untying her apron and reaching for us—me first, her hands on my cheeks and vanilla on her lips as she kissed me sweetly, and then Ava, whose back she patted.

"Good morning, my loves," she said with that smile of hers.

I shifted so Hannah could see her face. "Baby's hungry."

"Ah, come here, *leifje*," Hannah said as she scooped the baby up and cradled her.

Ava turned her face the second she realized where she was, mouth open and frantic. She squealed a frustrated cry.

Hannah smiled and bounced her, shushing her as she sat in one of the armchairs in the back corner and situated Ava, who squeaked and wriggled until she was happily suckling with Hannah's finger clutched in her fist.

I sat on the arm of the chair, and Hannah leaned into me.

"Tired?" I asked.

"Mmm," she hummed noncommittally and sighed dreamily. "Sometimes everything feels like a dream."

"She'll start sleeping better at night, and things will get easier."

Hannah looked up at me and smiled. "No, I mean you. This."

I cupped her cheek, thumbed her lip. "I promised you I'd do whatever I could to make you happy."

"And you told me I belonged with you."

"So what you're saying is, I'm right? Because I love to be right."

She laughed. "Yes, you were right. And I love you."

And as I looked down at her, I couldn't say the words back. I couldn't speak at all. So I kissed her instead, just like I'd kiss her a hundred thousand times, and every time, she'd know just how much I loved her.

Acknowledgments

To my husband Jeff — If moving to Holland wasn't hard enough, you took the burden and stress off my shoulders and carried it on your own, and you did it for me, for my career, for this book. There is no way to thank you for all you do, but I'll keep trying for as long as I live.

To Karla Sorensen — The exhaustive pestering, hair petting, and firefighting you endured through the composition of this book isn't just admirable and appreciated, it's saintly. No amount of Julia Quinn paperbacks, hugs, drinks, apologies or thanks will ever express how much you mean to me, to this story, and to my heart. I love you.

To Kandi Steiner — Thanks, Polly Pocket. I believe in myself mostly because you believe in me.

To Kyla Linde — One of my favorite things about moving to Europe is that we get to work together every day. Thank you for enduring my trillion voice messages as I work through my story and for allowing me to occasionally serenade you. You keep me sane daily.

To Emma Hart — If it weren't for your cheerleading and sprints and hugs and gifs and laughs, I probably wouldn't have made it through this intact.

To Corinne Michaels — Thank God I have you to hold my hand through all the massive changes. Your advice has helped me so much, given me peace of mind, and you have been my North Star. Thank you, thank you, thank you.

To Meghan March — Thank you so much for your lawyerly advice and your heart and your soul and your beautiful brain. I am so grateful to call you my friend.

To Christin Ostheimer — I love you, psycho. Your au pair insight was invaluable, and your tacos and rainbow glitter made everything just a little bit easier.

To my beta readers — You all saved my ass. You always do, but this time you saved me with exceptional swiftness and honesty.

To my editors, Jovana and Ellie — Thank you for squeezing me in to polish up my story at the very last minute. You are both so very appreciated.

To Lauren Perry — You work absolute magic. Thank you so much for always taking care of me.

And to my readers — Thank you so much for reading, for your love, for your support. Everything I do is for you, and I am forever humbled and grateful for each and every one of you.

About Staci

Staci has been a lot of things up to this point in her life: a graphic designer, an entrepreneur, a seamstress, a clothing and handbag designer, a waitress. Can't forget that. She's also been a mom to three little girls who are sure to grow up to break a number of hearts. She's been a wife, even though she's certainly not the cleanest, or the best cook. She's also super, duper fun at a party, especially if she's been drinking whiskey, and her favorite word starts with f, ends with k.

From roots in Houston, to a seven year stint in Southern California, Staci and her family ended up settling somewhere in between and equally north, in Denver. They are new enough that snow is still magical. When she's not writing, she's gaming, cleaning, or designing graphics.

follow staci hart:

Website: Stacihartnovels.com
Facebook: Facebook.com/stacihartnovels
Twitter: Twitter.com/imaquirkybird
Pinterest: pinterest.com/imaquirkybird

Made in the USA
Coppell, TX
22 June 2021